There was no time for a plan of attack, no time to even figure out what was going on.

Katherine screamed again, and Hunter's heart stopped dead in his chest. Swearing, he took the stairs two at a time to get to her.

Feeling like he was running in quicksand, it seemed to take him an eternity to reach the top of the stairs. Katherine didn't scream again, but that did little to reassure him. She couldn't scream if someone had knocked her out...or killed her.

Something squeezed his heart at the thought. No, dammit! She wasn't dead, and anyone who even thought about hurting her was going to have to deal with him.

Dear Reader,

I've heard of writers who write romance novels by formula: the hero and heroine meet by page 5, the first kiss is by page 50, the first love scene should begin by page 150, etc, etc. I don't do that. I have to let a story evolve and give the characters the space they need to come together. And my editor, thank God, indulges me! So sometimes the hero and heroine don't meet until the twenty-first page of the manuscript—as they do in *A Hero to Count On*—but it's worth the wait. Especially when you have a hero and heroine like Hunter Sinclair and Katherine Wyatt. I love the chemistry between them...and the sass. Writing their story was great fun, and I have to say that so far, this is my favorite of the BROKEN ARROW RANCH series. But then again, I feel that way about all my books when I finish them! I hope you do, too.

Enjoy!

Linda Turner

A HERO
TO COUNT ON

Linda Turner

Silhouette
Romantic
SUSPENSE

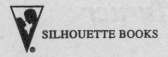

SILHOUETTE BOOKS

ISBN-13: 978-0-373-27578-6
ISBN-10:   0-373-27578-1

A HERO TO COUNT ON

Copyright © 2008 by Linda Turner

This edition published by arrangement with Harlequin Books S.A.

® and TM are trademarks of Harlequin Books S.A., used under license. Trademarks indicated with ® are registered in the United States Patent and Trademark Office, the Canadian Trade Marks Office and in other countries.

Visit Silhouette Books at www.eHarlequin.com

Printed in U.S.A.

Books by Linda Turner

Silhouette Romantic Suspense

‡*Gable's Lady* #523
‡*Cooper* #553
‡*Flynn* #572
‡*Kat* #590
Who's the Boss? #649
The Loner #673
Maddy Lawrence's Big Adventure #709
The Lady in Red #763
†*I'm Having Your Baby?!* #799
†*A Marriage-Minded Man?* #829
†*The Proposal* #847
†*Christmas Lone-Star Style* #895
**The Lady's Man* #931
**A Ranching Man* #992
**The Best Man* #1010
**Never Been Kissed* #1051
The Enemy's Daughter #1064
The Man Who Would Be King #1124
**Always a McBride* #1231
††*Deadly Exposure* #1304
††*Beneath the Surface* #1333
††*A Younger Man* #1423
††*Mission: M.D.* #1456
Fortune Hunter's Hero #1473
Under His Protection #1496
A Hero to Count On #1508

‡The Wild West
†The Lone Star Social Club
**Those Marrying McBrides!
††Turning Points
*Broken Arrow Ranch

LINDA TURNER

began reading romance novels in high school and began writing them one night when she had nothing else to read. She's been writing ever since. Single and living in Texas, she travels every chance she gets, scouting locales for her books.

Prologue

Lying in her boyfriend's arms, her heart still pounding from their loving, Katherine Wyatt felt like crying. How many evenings had they spent like this? After two years she couldn't remember. She just knew that, even though she loved Nigel with all her heart, she needed more from him than sex. "We need to talk," she said huskily.

"If this is about me breaking our date last weekend, I'm sorry, love, but I had to go to Paris again. There was a last-minute glitch in an acquisition, and the entire deal would have fallen through if I hadn't taken a personal hand in things. Don't be mad. I was just doing my job."

He was always "just doing his job." She tried to understand, but ever since she'd known him, Paris had been a problem. It seemed like every time they made plans to do something special, he had to travel to Paris to take care of some kind of glitch with the import/-export business he'd inherited from his father.

She tried, however, not to complain. She'd had boy-friends who couldn't keep a job, who didn't work, who expected her to loan them money. She never had to worry about that with Nigel. He not only worked hard, he always paid for everything when they were together and spoiled her with wonderful gifts. How could she find fault with that?

Considering all that, she knew she should have been happy. He was a wonderful man—generous and loving, affectionate, honest and kind. He was, in fact, everything she could want...except her husband.

"I want to get married."

The second she said the words, he stiffened. She wasn't surprised. She'd tried discussing marriage with him before, but every time the word came up, he found a way to change the subject. Not this time. She wanted a husband, children, a home with toys and dogs and a swing in the yard. If he wasn't interested in having the same thing, then she had some hard decisions to make about continuing their relationship.

"I know you swore you'd never get married again after your divorce, but I'm not Cynthia. I'm nothing like her. I'm not going to hurt you or take you to the cleaners—"

Setting her away from him, he reached for his pants. "It's not that."

"Then what is it?" she asked, hurt. "We've been dating for two years! I love you. I want to have your children while I'm still young enough to enjoy them."

"Sweetheart, you're only twenty-eight!"

"I'll be twenty-nine next month," she said. "I'm ready to settle down. If you're not, then at least give me some idea of when you will be. Give me some kind of hope."

For a moment she didn't think he was going to answer her. Pulling on his shirt, his face set in grim lines, he didn't look at her as he tucked in his shirt, then sat down to tug on his shoes and tie them. She'd never seen him so somber.

Suddenly chilled, without quite knowing why, she pulled on a robe and quickly belted it around her waist. Even then, she wasn't ready for what he had to say when she turned to face him.

"Cynthia's not my ex-wife," he said bluntly. "She's my wife. I lied when I told you we were divorced. We've been married for three years."

Stunned, she gasped. Married. He was *married?* "No! You can't be. You're lying."

"We have a home in Paris...and a one-year-old son. That's why I had to fly home last weekend. He was sick."

His words hit her like a knife in the heart. Horrified, she looked at him as if she'd never seen him before. "You had a son a year after you and I started sleeping together?"

"It wasn't planned, Katherine—"

"Do you think that matters?" she cried. "You're married! While your wife was pregnant, you were having sex with me. And you obviously don't see anything wrong with that."

"She didn't know. She never has to know. I wouldn't be telling you if you weren't pressing me to get married."

Stunned, Katherine couldn't believe he was serious.

"So it's all right for you to cheat on your wife and son and lie to me as long as you're the only one who knows the truth? Is that what you're saying?"

"No, of course not," he retorted, scowling. "But telling the truth isn't always the best policy. People get hurt…"

"So you're saying it's all right to lie?" When he didn't deny it, she looked at him in confusion. "I don't know you anymore. I'm beginning to wonder if I ever did. Who are you? How can you be so cold and unfeeling?"

"I never wanted to hurt you," he growled, stung. "You know that."

"You hurt me—and your wife and son—the first time you flirted with me. You betrayed us all when you had sex with me without telling me the truth."

"It wasn't just sex—"

"Of course it was," she snapped. "What else could it be? You vowed to love and honor another woman till death do you part."

"But—"

"Don't you dare say that didn't mean you couldn't love someone else," she cut in coldly. "The only person you love is yourself. Does your wife know who you are? Does she have a clue what kind of man you are?"

"She loves me," he retorted. "That's all she needs to know."

"No," she corrected him, "she loves the man she thinks you are. If she ever discovers the truth, she's going to hate your guts. Just like I do."

He winced, and reached for her. "Katherine, sweetheart, I know you're hurt, but don't do this. Give me a chance to make it up to you—"

"Get out!"

"Sweetheart—"

"We're done," she told him coldly. "There's nothing else to say." And without another word, she stepped over to the bedroom door and jerked it open. Left with no choice, he walked out. It wasn't until she heard him slam the front door of her flat that she let herself cry.

Chapter 1

"I still can't understand why you went to Scotland, of all places," Priscilla grumbled. "I know you wanted to get away from everything that reminded you of Nigel, but what's wrong with Nice?"

"France? Are you serious?"

On the other end of the phone, Priscilla winced. "Sorry. I wasn't thinking. Obviously, anything connected with France is out of the question. But there's always Monaco or Greece. Or Brazil. Now, there's a change of scene! You could find yourself one of those fantastically good-looking Brazilians and have a good time. Trust me, you'll forget all about Nigel. And who knows? The new guy might have a brother you can introduce me to. We could end up being sisters *and* sisters-in-law—"

"Will you stop? I'm not looking for a man and neither should you. They're nothing but bad news."

"They're not all like Nigel," Priscilla said.

"Really?" Katherine scoffed. "You couldn't swear that by me. Remember Sam? And Thomas? And don't forget Lucas. He was worse than Nigel. He took me home to meet his parents and forgot to mention the little fact that he had another girlfriend. His parents were totally confused."

"Jackass," her sister retorted. "If I could punch him and the others in the nose, you know I would. But it wouldn't change anything, and it certainly wouldn't make you feel better. The only thing that's going to do that is getting on with your life."

"I'm not jumping back into dating, Cilla. Not this time."

"Buck said the same thing, and so did Elizabeth, and look what happened. They both found love when they least expected it. You can, too."

"No, thank you," Katherine said, shuddering. "Just the thought of putting myself through that again turns my blood cold."

"You're cold because you're in Scotland," her sister said bluntly. "Has the sun even been out since you've been there? It hasn't, has it?"

"I didn't come for the sun," she reminded her. "I just wanted some time for myself."

"Time for what? To mourn? To slip into depression? Being alone now is the worst thing you can do. You need family. Why don't you go to Colorado and see Elizabeth and Buck?"

She had to admit, she'd thought about it. But then she remembered she wouldn't just be visiting her brother and sister. Buck had Rainey now, and Elizabeth was head-over-heels for John. Regretfully, she shook her head. "I can't. Everyone's in love there. I'd only bring them all down."

"Hogwash! They love you. And none of us want you to go through this alone. We're all here for you if you'll just let us."

Katherine knew she was right, but she didn't know if she was ready to face anyone. She felt like such an idiot for not seeing Nigel for the lying dog he really was. "I'll think about it," she promised. "Just give me some time."

Time was something she had plenty of, and Katherine should have used it to her advantage. After all, she had plenty to do. She was an illustrator for one of the most well-known publishers of children's books in England, and she'd brought her latest project with her. It was due in a month, and she would need every second of the next thirty days to finish her illustrations on time.

But three days after her telephone conversation with Priscilla, she still found it impossible to focus on her work. The silence of her own company was driving her mad, and just when she thought she was getting her emotions under control, images of Nigel would float through her head uninvited, and tears would once again flood her eyes. Scotland obviously wasn't working for her. She had to get out of there.

For all of thirty seconds she considered going to a tropical island far, far away, somewhere where the language and food were so foreign that she wouldn't think twice about *him*. In the end, however, she knew there was only one place where she would find solace, and that was the Broken Arrow Ranch, near Willow Bend, Colorado.

She hadn't spent much time at the ranch, and six months ago, when she and her sisters and brother had inherited the place from their long-lost American relative, Hilda Wyatt, leaving London for a cattle ranch in the wilds of Colorado was the last thing she'd thought she'd ever be interested in. It was too far away, too rugged, too different from the kind of life she'd led in England, and she'd wanted nothing to do with it. She had gladly let her brother, Buck, move to Colorado and she'd stayed in London.

Her feelings about the ranch, however, changed drastically when her family came under attack. And it was all Hilda Wyatt's fault. She hadn't left the ranch to them outright, with no strings attached. Instead, through the terms of her will, she'd required someone from the family to spend every night at the ranch for a year. Buck or Katherine and her sisters could be absent from the house for one night, but not for two in a row. If they failed to meet the requirements of the will, then the ranch would go to an unnamed heir.

Katherine appreciated the fact that Hilda respected family heritage enough to include her and her siblings in her will even though she'd never met them. She'd obviously wanted the British branch of the Wyatts to inherit the Broken Arrow, if possible.

Unfortunately, she'd probably never suspected that once the citizens of Willow Bend learned of the conditions of the will and the unnamed heir, they would attack the legal heirs in order to drive them away from the ranch

so someone else could inherit. They'd harassed Buck and
Rainey, made their lives miserable. Then, while the new-
lyweds were gone on their honeymoon, someone had ter-
rorized Elizabeth when she'd taken Buck's place at the
ranch. If John, the ranch foreman, hadn't been there to
protect her—and fall in love with her—she could easily
have been seriously hurt, even killed, during her stay at
the ranch. Someone had shot out the windshield of the
vehicle she was driving and even set the hunting cabin
she and John had escaped to on fire.

Over the past few weeks, however, things had calmed
down considerably at the ranch, which wasn't surpris-
ing. Buck and Rainey had returned home from their honeymoon, and Elizabeth and John were engaged and busy
rebuilding the cabin where they would live once they
were married. When she arrived, three-fourths of the
family would be in residence. Surely, whoever was after
the ranch would realize that their odds of driving the
Wyatts away from the Broken Arrow were slim to none.

She would, she decided, be safe…and have thousands of acres to lose herself in and forget Nigel. The
decision made, she booted up her computer and booked
the first available flight to Colorado.

"What do you mean you need someone to pick you
up?" Elizabeth asked, shocked. "Where *are* you?"

"Changing planes in New York." Katherine laughed.
"I'm scheduled to arrive at four in Willow Bend. You
can pick me up, can't you?"

Surprised, Elizabeth said, "What? Oh, yes, of
course." Her thoughts on the wedding she and John
were scheduled to attend at three-thirty, she didn't have

a clue how they would get there on time to pick her up, but she could hardly tell Katherine that. She'd been through too much lately—the last thing Elizabeth wanted her to think was that her arrival was an inconvenience. "Everything's kind of crazy today, but someone will be there. Are you okay? Priscilla said you were in Scotland."

"I was. I just needed a complete change of scene. But I need family, too," she added huskily. "I don't want to be alone anymore."

At the sound of her sister's voice thick with pain, Elizabeth wanted to cry. "I know it hurts, but give it some time. Things will get better."

"I know," she choked. "I'll see you this afternoon. All right? I've got to go."

She hung up almost immediately, and Elizabeth didn't doubt for a minute that her sister was crying her eyes out. Her heart aching for her, she hurried into the dining room, where the rest of the family was lingering over an early lunch.

"Who was that?" Buck asked as Elizabeth took a seat across from her fiancé, John. "I've been expecting a call from Luke Hucklebee about the livestock trailer he's selling—"

"Katherine's in New York," she said. "She decided Scotland wasn't the right place for her, after all."

"Thank God for that," Rainey said. "What time's her plane getting in?"

"Four."

"Four!" Buck repeated, frowning. "But we won't be back from the cattle auction. And you and John will still—"

"Be at the wedding," she finished for him. "I know."

"We could leave the auction early," Rainey suggested. "Someone needs to be there to pick her up."

"I agree," Elizabeth said, "but I don't see how John and I can just walk out in the middle of the wedding. Unless, of course, we leave between the wedding and the reception, make a quick trip to the airport and bring her back with us to the reception."

"Oh, I don't think that would be a very good idea," Rainey said. "The last thing she's going to want to go to right now is a wedding."

"True, but what else can we do? After all the cows we lost to rustlers, you and Buck really need to go to the auction and pick up some calves—"

"I'll go."

When everyone at the dining room table turned to him in surprise, John's half brother, Hunter Sinclair, grinned crookedly. "Did you think I meant the auction? No, thanks—Buck and Rainey can handle that. I don't know one end of a cow from another. I was talking about Katherine. I'll pick her up at the airport."

"Are you sure?" Elizabeth asked him. "I thought you were going to Aspen."

"I can do that anytime," he assured her. "I don't mind. Really."

Studying him, Elizabeth still hesitated. Hunter had only been at the ranch a few days, but she'd recognized him for who he was within the first twenty minutes of his unexpected arrival. A flirt and a tease. He was too good-looking for his own good, and he could sweet-talk a woman without even thinking twice about it. That was the last thing Katherine needed right now.

"I appreciate the offer, Hunter, but Katherine's been having a difficult time lately. She's not going to be very good company—it would probably be better if either Buck or I picked her up."

"You mean because of that louse she was dating," he said. "He broke her heart and now she doesn't want anything to do with men."

"Well, I don't know that for sure, but she's been crying a lot. You shouldn't have to deal with that—"

"I'll handle her with kid gloves," he promised. "Honest. I know better than to take on a woman who's just found out the man she gave her heart to is a rat. She's safe with me. I'll treat her like my sister. Scout's honor."

"You don't have a sister," John pointed out, grinning. "And as far as I know, you were never a Scout."

"I could have been," he retorted with twinkling eyes. "I will be in my next lifetime. And I'll have a sister, too. Okay?"

"Yeah, right," his brother chuckled. "You'll probably pester the hell out of her, God help her. Elizabeth just wants to make sure you don't do that to Katherine."

"Me? C'mon, you know I'm a sweetheart. I'm certainly not going to pester Katherine. She's Elizabeth's sister, for heaven's sake. I've got to keep peace in the family. So go to your friends' wedding. I know you've both been looking forward to it, though God knows why. Why people celebrate when they're making the biggest mistake of their lives—"

"Hunter—"

He grinned at Rainey's warning tone. "Okay, okay. Each of you Wyatt women has the soul of a romantic.

That's another reason Katherine's safe with me. Unlike you guys, I'm not going anywhere near that."

Far from offended, Buck only chuckled. "Don't knock it until you've tried it."

"Yeah, come on in," John teased. "The water's fine."

"No, thanks. I prefer to be footloose and fancy-free and only answer to me. The only reason I'm offering to pick up Katherine is because you all have plans. I don't. But if you don't want me to…"

"Oh, no, it isn't that," Elizabeth assured him. "If you're sure you don't mind…and you won't flirt with her…you would really be helping us out."

"Then it's decided," he said promptly. "All of you go do what you have to do and I'll take care of Katherine. Don't worry. I'll make sure she's fine. Okay?"

Elizabeth knew he wouldn't deliberately hurt Katherine or make her feel uncomfortable. If he could make her laugh after all the tears she'd shed, then she would kiss him for it when she and John got back from the wedding.

"Okay," she sighed, relieved. "I've got a picture of her from Buck's wedding that's great. You can take it with you so you won't have to ask every woman who steps off the plane if they're Katherine."

"Damn," he retorted, wicked mischief dancing in his eyes. "That was the part I was looking forward to the most."

Standing just past the security check at Willow Bend's small regional airport, Hunter didn't really need the picture that Elizabeth had loaned him to recognize her sister. After all, this was Willow Bend, for heaven's sake, not Chicago. If there were more than a handful of passengers getting off the plane, he'd be damned surprised. And Katherine was British and had two sisters that were in the fashion industry. If she dressed as stylishly as Elizabeth, recognizing her wasn't going to be a problem.

But even as he assured himself he'd know her the second he saw her, his gaze once again dropped to the picture he'd looked at at least ten times in nearly as many minutes. She was cute. Great smile, heart-shaped face, dimples. And the mischief that danced in her big blue eyes would make more than one man stop and take a second look at her. She could, no doubt, be trouble with a capital *T.* And there was nothing he liked more than a woman he could get into trouble with.

If you're sure you don't mind...and you won't flirt with her...

Elizabeth's words echoed in his ears, along with his own. *I'll take care of Katherine. Don't worry. She'll be fine.*

Swallowing a groan, he wanted to kick himself. Idiot! What possessed him to say such a thing? He hadn't even seen her picture yet. Not, he acknowledged ruefully, that he had any intention of making a serious play for the woman. She was extended family, of a sorts. Or she would be when her sister married his half brother. And he didn't play around with women who were closely connected to friends or family. That only created hard feelings when the women discovered he wasn't the marrying kind.

So Katherine Wyatt was off-limits and had been before he'd even seen her picture. Damn. He could have had some fun with her. Instead he had to behave himself. Sometimes life just wasn't fair.

Grinning at the thought, he looked up as passengers started down the escalator that led to the baggage-claim area; and there was Katherine Wyatt, right in the middle of the pack. She'd been crying—that much was obvious—and the sparkle was gone from her eyes. In spite of that, all he could think was that her picture didn't do her justice.

How could a woman who looked as if she'd cried all the way across the Atlantic and halfway through the flight from New York look so pretty? She'd been on a plane for hours, but you wouldn't know it to look at her. Her chestnut hair was a mass of long curls that were held back from her face with a blue-and-white polka-dot scarf, and the red T-shirt and white jeans that she wore didn't have a single wrinkle. If her eyes were swollen from crying, that was the only crack in her armor. She stood tall, all five-foot-two of her, in wedge-soled sandals, and was the cutest handful of trouble he'd seen in a long time.

"And she's off-limits," he muttered, swallowing a groan.

Resigned, he pushed away from the wall he was leaning against and headed toward Katherine as she stepped off the escalator. Her attention on the signs that directed passengers to the baggage-claim area, she didn't spare him a glance.

Frowning, he couldn't believe she was so unaware of her surroundings. Considering all the attacks against her family and the ranch over the past six months, she should have been on constant guard. Didn't she know she was in danger? He'd have to talk to her about that on the way back to the ranch.

Stepping forward to help her with the heavy carry-on bag she had slung over her shoulder, he said easily, "You must be Katherine. Here…let me help you with that."

Chapter 2

Caught off guard, Katherine turned sharply, just in time to see a stranger reach for her bag. Alarmed, she wrapped protective fingers around the shoulder strap of her carry-on and took a quick step back. "What do you think you're doing?" she demanded, scowling.

"Don't get all spooked on me," he said with a crooked grin as he once again reached for her bag. "I'm just trying to help—"

Outraged, she knocked his hand away. "I don't know who the hell you think you are, but you've got two seconds to get away from me or I'm calling security!"

Her threat should have sent him packing. Instead he only laughed. "C'mon, there's no need for that. I'm harmless."

"Yeah, right," she scoffed.

She'd never seen a man who looked less harmless in her life. He was a bad boy—she could see it in his wicked, laughing green eyes—and she didn't doubt for a second that he could melt a woman's bones without ever touching her. She wanted nothing to do with him.

Deliberately she turned her back on him. "I don't need your help. Leave me alone."

"Okay, if that's the way you want it. It's ten miles to the ranch, but if you want to walk, far be it from me to stop you. Elizabeth's going to kill me, but, hey, I tried."

"I don't care—" she began, only to break off abruptly at the mention of her sister. Whirling, she studied him suspiciously. "How do you know Elizabeth? Who *are* you?"

"Hunter Sinclair," he retorted. When she just looked at him blankly, he explained, "I'm John's brother. He and Elizabeth couldn't make it, so I volunteered to pick you up, instead."

At his words, Katherine paled. "John doesn't have a brother. And I just talked to my sister this morning, and she never once mentioned that she was sending anyone to pick me up. They sent you, didn't they?"

Confused, he frowned. "*They?* They who? Who are you talking about?"

"The thugs who want the ranch," she retorted. "Did you think I don't know about what's been going on just because I live in England? Elizabeth and Buck keep me posted on everything. They told me who they trust, and trust me, your name never came up. So get the hell away from me. If you lay so much as a finger on me, I'm going to scream my guts out and I won't stop until somebody throws your butt in jail."

Impressed—she was tougher than she looked—he

stepped back, raising his hands to show he meant no harm. "Whoa, whoa! There's no need to scream. I'm not going to hurt you. John does have a brother. A half brother."

"Then why hasn't he mentioned you?"

"How the hell do I know? Because I'm the black sheep of the family?" He shrugged. "Maybe. Maybe because we haven't seen each other in years and lost touch. Maybe my name just didn't come up when you talked to him. You'll have to ask him yourself."

"I'll do that," she snapped, and reached for her phone.

"You won't get him," he warned. "He and Elizabeth went to a wedding. It started at three-thirty. That's why they sent me."

Ignoring him, she punched in her sister's number, then John's. Neither one answered. Was he telling the truth? she wondered as her eyes searched his. He had all the right answers, but she couldn't forget how badly certain people in Willow Bend wanted to drive her family away from the ranch. What if this man was part of that conspiracy? What if he'd somehow grabbed Elizabeth and John and locked them up somewhere for a couple of days? If he could lure everyone away from the ranch for forty-eight hours, the struggle to hang on to the Broken Arrow would be over for good.

"I'm not going anywhere with you until I talk to John and Elizabeth first," she said flatly, "so you might as well get comfortable."

"Fine by me," he said with a shrug. "I've got nothing but time. And we can get to know each other. Do you still read tea leaves?"

Surprised, she blinked. "I beg your pardon?"

"Your grandmother taught you to read tea leaves when you were a little girl, didn't she? I heard you were really good at it."

"Who—"

"Elizabeth said you found a watch she lost on a school field trip. It was near a fountain, wasn't it? It slipped off her arm when she threw some pennies in the fountain."

No one but her family knew that story. Stunned, Katherine didn't have to ask where he'd heard it. Elizabeth must have told him, just as he'd claimed.

"I understand why you don't trust me," Hunter said quietly. "After everything that's happened to Buck and Rainey and Elizabeth, I'd be spooked, too, if I were you. But I'm not your enemy. You have nothing to fear from me. I won't hurt you."

The teasing glint that had been in his eyes just moments before was gone, and there was no doubting his sincerity. She wanted to believe him, but lately her family had learned the hard way not to trust anyone. "I still need to talk to Elizabeth," she said huskily as she once again reached for her phone. "As soon as she verifies you're really who claim you are, we can go."

"Have it your way," he said with a shrug. "I'm willing to wait as long as you are. How about a cup of coffee while we wait? Or would you rather have tea? Hot tea's not something you're going to run into in this neck of the woods, but there's bound to be something. Let's see what we can scrounge up."

Katherine didn't really want tea—or for Hunter Sinclair to be nice to her. She just wanted some time to herself. But if Hunter was telling the truth—and there was every indication that he was—they were, in some convoluted way, extended family, and the least she could do was be polite.

Before they could find coffee or tea, however, her phone rang, and with a sigh of relief, she snatched it up. "Elizabeth? Thank God! I was afraid you wouldn't call me back for hours."

"We just walked out of the church and are on our way to the reception. Are you home yet? Did Hunter have any trouble recognizing you? I loaned him a picture—"

"Oh, he had a much easier time than I did. I was expecting *you*. Why didn't you tell me you couldn't make it?"

"You were in the air," her sister reminded her, "so I couldn't reach you on your cell. You caught me off guard when you called—John and I had a wedding to go to, but after everything you've been through, I didn't want you to think we didn't want you here. So when Hunter volunteered to pick you up, it seemed like the perfect solution." Struck by a sudden thought, she said sharply, "Everything's all right, isn't it? He promised to behave himself."

Aware of Hunter's eyes on her as he waited for her to finish her conversation, she stiffened. *Behave himself?* Had Elizabeth asked him to behave himself with her? Why? Had the two of them discussed her?

Dozens of questions—and answers she didn't like—bombarded her, but all she said was, "Everything's fine, now that I know he's who he claimed to be. I didn't know John had a brother."

"I just found out myself last week when he showed up at the ranch," Elizabeth said. "But he's a great guy.

He may tease you until you want to shoot him, but John trusts him completely, and you can, too."

"If you say so," she said, studying Hunter doubtfully. "I'll let you know."

"Be nice," Elizabeth laughed. "I'll see you in a couple of hours."

When Katherine hung up, she wasn't surprised to find Hunter grinning at her. "You don't have to look so smug," she sniffed, refusing to be embarrassed for distrusting him. "She said you were a tease but I could trust you. I'm reserving judgment."

"On what? Whether I'm a tease or that you can trust me?"

Looking down her pert nose at him, she lifted a delicately arched brow. "What do you think?"

Far from offended, he only laughed. "And here I thought I was doing so well. What is it with you cute ones? None of you will give me the time of day."

Fighting a grin, she pointedly looked at her watch. "It's four-twenty."

"Smart-ass," he chuckled as he opened the door to his Toyota 4Runner for her and helped her into the vehicle. "I knew you were going to be trouble the second I laid eyes on you."

"I'm sure I don't know what you're talking about."

"Yeah, right." Shutting her door for her, he walked around the vehicle and climbed into the driver's seat, his grin maddening as he reminded her to buckle up. The second her seat belt was safely in place, he glanced behind him, threw the transmission into Reverse and hit the gas.

"What the—?" Grabbing the handhold on the doorframe, she gasped, "Are you mad?"

"You mean crazy?" he laughed as he put the SUV in Drive and head for the highway. "Sometimes. I don't let any grass grow under my feet."

"Somehow, that doesn't surprise me," she retorted dryly. "So what's a man like you doing in Colorado?"

"Taking a break between jobs. I don't start my new job in L.A. until next month, so it seemed like a good time to visit John."

Her gaze on the road that stretched out before them as he headed for the ranch, she said, "I thought it was a good time for a visit, too."

"Because you wanted to put some space between you and that amoral jackass you were involved with?" At her sharp look of surprise, he added, "Oh, yeah, I know about it. And just for the record, you should have known better than to trust the bastard."

"Oh, really?" Indignant, she said, "And how would you know that? You don't know anything about Nigel."

"I know he's a man," he retorted. "That's all I need to know. Even a woman with a pea brain should know better than to trust a man."

"I beg your pardon! I know a lot of good men."

"Really? Name two."

She held up her index finger. "My brother." Then a second finger. "*Your* brother."

"Most men aren't like your brother or mine," he returned. "Or haven't you figured that out yet?"

"Are you including yourself in that group?"

"Guilty as charged," he said promptly. "We're after only one thing. You should know that. The jerk you were in love with didn't just lie to you—he lied to his wife, too, and cheated on both of you. Talk about a scumbag. If you were smart, you'd never have anything to do with a man again."

"Trust me," she said stiffly, "I learned my lesson. That's exactly what I intend to do."

"Yeah, yeah," he mocked. "That's what all you women say. Then some good-looking loser flirts with you, you get all hot and bothered and think you've found Prince Charming. Why does everything have to be a fairy tale? What's wrong with good old-fashioned sex for sex's sake?"

"You're a cynic."

He didn't deny it. "Yeah. So?"

"You don't believe in love?"

"Not hardly," he said with a short laugh. "It's all just hormones."

Deep down inside, Katherine's bruised heart was tempted to agree with him. If she didn't believe in love, she reasoned, she couldn't get hurt. It made perfect sense. There was only one small problem. If she didn't believe in love, why did she feel as if her heart had been ripped out of her chest by Nigel?

"I don't think so," she said quietly. "Hormones don't hurt like this."

Cringing at the sound of the pain thickening her voice, she knew she was going to cry if they didn't change the subject. "Enough doom and gloom," she said briskly, straightening her shoulders. "So you're the half brother. What's your story? It has to be more entertaining than mine."

"I don't know about that," he said wryly. "I can always make something up. My mother always said I could tell a better story than all the other kids put together."

"And how many *kids* were there in your family?"

"Eight."

"Eight! Are you serious?"

Grinning, he shrugged. "Doesn't everybody have eight brothers and sisters? Of course, some are step, others half, a few full blood. Between them, my parents were married five times." At her look of horror, he chuckled. "It's pretty damn awful, isn't it? My mom married twice, my dad three times, and they're probably not done. They're both currently divorced and looking. Talk about optimists. They're both crazy."

"So that's why you're such a cynic. No wonder you don't believe in happily ever after."

"You're damn straight," he retorted. "There's no such thing."

Katherine had always considered herself a die-hard romantic, but that was before…before Nigel lied to her, before he made a fool of her, before he charmed her into falling in love with him without even hinting that he was married. "If you're hoping for an argument, you're out of luck," she said flatly. "I just got my heart stomped on by a man who claimed to love me. If that's love, I want no part of it."

She meant every word, but later, after they arrived at the ranch and Hunter carried her luggage upstairs, and she'd gone down to the kitchen to make a pot of tea, the silent emptiness of the house made her more lonely than ever. She found herself thinking of Nigel, and she hated it. She had to stop this! The man was a rat, and even if he'd contacted her and told her he'd made a mistake—*she* was the one he loved—she would have told him never to darken her doorstep again. So why did her heart ache? Why did she constantly feel like crying? Why couldn't she get past—

"You're thinking of him again, aren't you?"

Looking up from her thoughts to find Hunter standing in the kitchen doorway, watching her, she frowned in irritation. "Do you always slink around the house that way, spying on people?"

Not the least apologetic, he laughed. "Yeah. Does it bother you?"

"Yes," she retorted. "At least have the decency to knock, to let someone know you're there."

His green eyes alight with mischief, he lifted his fist and knocked twice on the doorway.

She told herself she wasn't going to laugh. But he didn't make it easy, darn him! Trying and failing to give him a stern frown, she sniffed, "Very funny. How long did it take you to think that one up?"

"Sweetheart, you just bring out the best in me," he drawled, winking at her.

The sound of a car honking in the drive suddenly echoed through the house. "That must be Elizabeth and John," Katherine said. Thankful for the distraction—the man was far too sure of himself—she quickly set down the cup of tea she'd just made for herself. "They're early."

Hurrying out to greet them, she took one look at the two of them together and found it hard not to believe in love. Her sister was glowing, and John couldn't seem to take his eyes off her.

"Look at you!" she told Elizabeth, stepping back from a hug to study her with a teasing smile. "You look wonderful."

"It's the dress," she said, grinning as she showed off

the ultrafeminine pink concoction Katherine recognized as their sister Priscilla's design. "Cilla outdid herself."

"True," Katherine agreed, "but it's not the dress. Have you set a date yet for the wedding?" When her sister hesitated, she said quietly, "It's okay, Lizzie. You're getting married. I'm happy for you."

"I could kick Nigel," Elizabeth retorted, scowling. "Somebody needs to go to Paris and string him up by his ears."

"Just say the word, and I'll go," Hunter volunteered as he joined them. "The bastard needs to be taught a lesson."

"I'll go with you," John added. "After we get through with the jerk, he'll think twice before he cheats on his wife and takes advantage of another woman."

Amazed by the three of them, Katherine couldn't help but smile. "You all have been in the Wild West too long," she told her sister. "Where's Buck? Don't we need him to ride shotgun?"

"He and Rainey have gone to an auction in Colorado Springs. And trust me, if he thought for one second that he could confront Nigel, he'd already be packing for Paris," Elizabeth said, sobering. "We're all outraged by what he did to you. He's nothing but a lying, two-timing adulterer, and don't you dare lose a second's sleep over the jerk. You deserve better. Give it time. You'll find someone."

"Oh, no!" she cried. "I'm not going there again, thank you very much. I'd rather deal with mad cow than take on another man."

"Whoa!" John said quickly, horrified. "This is ranching country. Don't say that!"

"Sorry," she said with a grimace. "I didn't mean that,

of course. The cows don't deserve to suffer just because Nigel was and is and always will be a bastard."

She would have sworn she was in perfect control, but tears suddenly stung her eyes, and before she could blink them away, Elizabeth saw her distress and came to her rescue. "What are we doing, standing in the drive, when you've got to be exhausted? Let's go inside and have a spot of tea."

"I just made some."

"Good. I made a pound cake yesterday—it's Hilda's recipe. We'll have that, too."

Rainey and Buck came in later that evening. Except for Priscilla, the family was finally together again. It didn't take Katherine long to realize that coming to Colorado had been the right decision, after all. Over the course of the next few days, she fell into a routine of having meals with the family, then retreating to quiet, private areas of the ranch to work on her illustrations. For the most part, she thought she was doing quite well. She'd gotten her emotions under control, and if she cried, it was only when she was alone in bed at night.

She hid it well—or so she thought—until she was forced to face the truth one morning at the breakfast table. "You've been crying again," Buck said flatly.

"I have not!"

"And you're losing weight," Elizabeth added with a frown. "You need to eat more than an apple for breakfast."

"I do! I had—"

"Toast," Rainey finished for her when she hesitated. "One lousy piece of toast. That's not enough to keep a bird alive."

"I've never been a big eater…"

"Oh, really?" Elizabeth retorted. "It seems to me that I remember someone eating an entire batch of scones with butter and honey. And then there's Mother's recipe for braised lamb. You used to eat *three* servings!"

"I did not! It was—"

"Four," Buck said with a quick grin. "I distinctly remember."

Trapped, knowing her siblings' memories were every bit as sharp as her own, she laughed. "All right. So I have a weakness for braised lamb and hot scones—"

"You mean biscuits," John teased.

"They were made and eaten in England," she said loftily. "That makes them scones."

"And you ate a whole pan of them?" Hunter said with a lazy grin. Seated across the breakfast table from her, he surveyed her with new respect. "I'm impressed. Who knew a skinny little thing like you could eat so much?"

Her chin jutted up at that. "I'm not skinny. I just have a high metabolism."

"Yeah, right," he chuckled.

When she gave him a narrow-eyed look that would have sent a lesser man scurrying for cover, Elizabeth quickly jumped into the conversation. "I think you need to get out more, circulate, meet people. We should have a party."

"And introduce her to all the jerks who've been trying to drive us off the ranch?" Buck drawled. "I don't think so."

"Good," Katherine retorted. "I don't want a party."

"How about a dating service?" Rainey suggested.

"An online one would give you the chance to meet someone from other areas."

"No!"

"It could be fun," Hunter pointed out. "If you like losers—"

"Hunter!"

"Stop that!"

"Just because someone uses a dating service doesn't mean they're a loser."

Hardly hearing the defense of her family, Katherine frowned at him in irritation. She didn't know what it was about him that rubbed her the wrong way, but every time their eyes met, he knew just what to say to raise her hackles. And he knew exactly what he was doing. The knowledge was right there in his laughing eyes.

Sitting back in her chair, she surveyed him with a frown. "When are you leaving? Surely it's time for you to move on to your job in California. If you like, I can help you pack."

Far from offended, he only grinned. "I don't know. I kind of like it here. I thought I might stay awhile, if that's okay."

When she gave him a withering look, John said dryly, "This is great. One big, happy family. Don't you just love it?"

Hunter Sinclair was, Katherine decided three days later, the biggest pest she'd ever met. After his annoying comments at breakfast on Saturday, she'd done everything she could to avoid him, without success. If she hadn't known better, she would have sworn he had radar where she was concerned. Whenever she slipped off by herself, he always seemed to show up.

She still didn't know how he'd known she was at the ranch's hot springs yesterday. She'd taken her sketchpad and pencils and slipped away from the homestead in Rainey's SUV. All she'd told Rainey was that she was going out on the ranch somewhere to work on the illustrations that were due at the end of the month. No one had seen her leave the homestead, let alone followed her. Considering that, she should have had the rest of the morning to herself. Instead, she'd hardly settled beside the bubbling hot springs when Hunter drove up in his Toyota 4Runner.

"What are you doing here?"

Not the least bit put off by her greeting, he'd only grinned and started toward her with the lazy grace of a mountain lion on the prowl. "I was just out exploring and decided to check out the springs," he said easily. "Buck told me the Indians used to camp here."

It was a good story, and another woman might have swallowed it without a blink of an eye. But thanks to Nigel, she wasn't nearly as naive as she'd once been. "Really? And you just happened to show up when I was here?"

"That's right," he chuckled. "Coincidence is a pretty amazing thing, isn't it?"

"Coincidence, my eye," she retorted. "You followed me!"

"Now, sweetheart, why would I do that?"

"Don't call me sweetheart!"

"Yes, ma'am. What would you like me to call you? Personally I like darlin'. It's got a nice ring, you know.

But I can't call you that without kissing you first. That's one of my rules—"

Frustrated, irritated, fighting the smile that tugged at her lips, she hadn't said another word. She'd packed up her art supplies and left.

When he'd gone out last night to one of the local watering holes, she'd told herself she was glad. There was bound to be a woman there who would catch—and keep—his attention for the rest of his stay at the ranch. Then he would stop yanking her chain and pestering her.

Clinging to that thought, she should have slept the night away. Instead, the darn man chased her into her dreams, and she'd tossed and turned and stared at the ceiling for hours before finally falling asleep around four in the morning.

Not surprisingly, the rest of the family, including Hunter, had already eaten breakfast by the time she woke at ten, and the house was deserted. Desperate for a cup of tea, she stepped into the kitchen, only to discover a note from Elizabeth on the refrigerator.

Hey, sleepyhead. Hope you slept well. John and I have gone to the cabin, and Buck and Rainey and Hunter are riding fence on the ranch's north boundary. If you want some company, take the dirt road west of the barn and it'll take you to the cabin. I packed a picnic lunch for the three of us, and Rainey left her keys for you on the kitchen table. See you later. Elizabeth.

So Hunter was with Buck and Rainey. She shouldn't have been relieved—she liked to think she didn't care what Hunter Sinclair did one way or the other—but she couldn't forget the way his eyes danced when he teased her. Why did he have to be so attractive? Why did she have to notice?

Irritated with herself—she really did need a break from the man!—she grabbed the keys and found Rainey's SUV parked in the circular drive at the front of the house. Within minutes she was heading west, toward the old hunting cabin in the mountains where Elizabeth and John would live after they were married.

Nearly forty-five minutes later, she broke through the trees into a small, natural clearing, and there was the cabin right in front of her. Last month, one of the wannabe heirs had torched it in an effort to drive Elizabeth and John away from the ranch, and the damage had been significant. When Elizabeth had told her that she and John were going to rebuild it and make it their home, Katherine had thought they were crazy. She'd assumed it was nothing but a burned-out shell and any attempt to repair it would be nothing but a waste of time and money. She couldn't have been more wrong.

Only part of the cabin had been burned, and John had already removed the damaged wood and replaced it. He hadn't, however, stopped there. The framework for two new rooms and a new front and back porch were already in place, and although the design was simple, Katherine could see that it was going to be charming when it was finished.

"Hey, stranger, I see you finally decided to join the world of the living," her sister said with a grin as she parked and stepped from the car. "What do you think?"

"It's wonderful! Why didn't you tell me..."

From the corner of her eye, she caught sight of movement and turned just in time to see Hunter come around the side of the cabin. Stunned, she gasped, "What's *he* doing here?"

Chapter 3

He'd pulled off his shirt and hung it on a nearby tree branch, and in the late-morning sun, his bare chest glistened with sweat. Transfixed, Katherine heard a roar in her ears and only then realized that it was the thunder of her heart. And it was all Hunter's fault, she decided with a scowl.

No man had a right to look so good dressed in nothing but a pair of worn jeans. Faded, torn, soft from a thousand or more washes, they hugged his lean hips in a way that any woman with any sense of decency would have wanted nothing to do with. And all she could think about was touching him. Were the muscles of his chest as hard as his jeans were soft?

Shocked by the direction of her thoughts, she wanted to sink right through the ground. Her eyes met his, and the glint of humor she saw there told her without words that he knew exactly what he was doing to her. And he loved it.

Hot color flooding her cheeks, she hardly heard her sister say, "You mean Hunter? When he heard that John was working on the roof today, he offered to help."

"I don't know what we would have done without him," John added from the roof.

"I told you I was a good guy to have around," Hunter told Katherine with a grin. "Wanna help?"

Help him? She didn't think so. "Thanks, but I don't like heights."

"Then you'd better get some Dramamine or something," he said with a wicked chuckle, "because you're going to need it when I take you to the moon and back."

"Hunter!" Elizabeth gasped, laughing. "Stop that!"

Up on the roof, John grinned broadly. "He's just giving her fair warning, honey."

"I don't need fair warning," Katherine retorted, never taking her eyes from Hunter's. "In other words, Romeo, I'm not interested."

"Are you sure?" he teased. "You don't know what you're missing."

"I'll chance it," she said dryly. "I know that must devastate you, but there's nothing wrong with your ego. You'll survive."

"I might grow on you."

"You mean...like a fungus? I don't think so."

"Katherine!" Elizabeth choked on a laugh. "Remember your manners."

"Leave her alone," John said, grinning. "She's holding her own."

"She sure is," Hunter chuckled. "Be still my heart."

Determined not to smile, Katherine said, "You're wasting your time here, lover boy. Why don't you check out Mabel at the Rusty Bucket? Last I heard, she was hot for just about any cowboy who walked in the door."

"Katherine!"

"It's okay, Elizabeth," Hunter chuckled. "The woman's crazy about me. Can't you tell?"

Katherine just looked down her nose at him. "Don't let me keep you from your work," she said coolly. "I have better things to do than drool over you."

Not the least insulted, he only laughed and made his way up the ladder to help John.

Long after Katherine returned to the house, the memory of Hunter dressed in nothing but jeans, work boots and a grin still had the power to make her mouth go dry. And it was driving her crazy. What was wrong with her? It had only been a few weeks since she'd discovered that the man she'd planned to spend the rest of her life with was not only married to another woman but had a child with her. He'd broken her heart in a way no one ever had before, and it would be months, possibly years, before she was ready to move on.

So why did Hunter only have to grin at her to set her heart pounding?

She needed a distraction, she decided. She had work, of course, but she needed something more than her illustrations, something that would keep her thoughts from straying to Hunter's worn jeans and hard body whenever she dropped her guard. But what? she wondered with a frown. How was she supposed to put him out of her head?

She thought about it for the rest of the day but couldn't come up with anything. Then she sat down to dinner with the rest of the family and once again found herself seated across from Hunter. He took one look at her and winked, and suddenly she knew what she had to do.

"You should have stuck around this morning," Hunter told her with a grin. "What'd you do the rest of the day? Miss me?"

"Not at all," she said dryly. "Instead, I've been giving it some thought, and I've decided Elizabeth and Rainey were right. I need to join a dating service."

"Are you serious?"

"That's wonderful!"

"Are you sure you want to do that?" Buck asked with a frown as his wife and sister voiced their approval. "There's no way to check these guys out."

"Buck's right," Hunter said, scowling. "You think you had trouble with your married boyfriend? Wait till you meet a con man who takes a woman for everything he can get while he tricks her into falling in love with him. Men like that feed on women like you online."

"What do you mean...'women like me'?" she demanded indignantly. "I'm not some naive innocent who's never been out on my own before. I know a line when I hear one."

"Really? Then why did you believe Mr. Wonderful when he told you he loved you? If he really loved you, why's he in Paris with his wife?"

"Hunter!"

Katherine waved off her sister. His words hurt, but she knew Hunter was right. "I made a mistake," she said bluntly. "I won't do it again."

"How do you know that? Married men are smooth talkers, and an on-line dating service is perfect for them. They tell you women anything they want, charm you, and you fall in love before you even see the whites of their eyes."

"Maybe some women do, but I don't!"

"Sure you do. Don't take it personal. All women are patsies when it comes to smooth talkers. You just can't help yourself. You're a woman."

Narrowing her eyes at him, she studied him in irritation. Why did he always sit directly across the table from her? Every time she looked up, she was looking right at him. "And you're a man. Does that mean you're a male chauvinist p—"

"Katherine! That's no way to treat a guest."

"Let her be," John chuckled when Elizabeth sent her sister a reproving frown. "He asked for it."

Sitting back in his chair, Hunter grinned across the table at Katherine. "Why am I a chauvinist when I'm just trying to warn you about some loser looking to take advantage of you?"

"Because you're implying that women are so foolish that they need a keeper," she retorted. "I can take care of myself, thank you very much, and so can Elizabeth and Rainey."

"Did I say you couldn't?"

"No, but you implied—"

"I'm a pretty up-front guy, Kitty-Kat. If I thought you were incompetent, you'd know it."

Just as he'd expected, she stiffened at the nickname. "My name is Katherine," she told him coldly.

Damn, she was easy to tease. Making no effort to hold back a grin, he said, "I like Kitty-Kat better. It's got a ring to it, don't you think?"

"When did you say you were leaving?"

"I'll let you know," he promised, chuckling.

He didn't, in fact, intend to go anywhere anytime soon. There was no job in California. He worked for himself as a private investigator, though no one here knew that, not even John. He'd intended to tell him, but when John called him to tell him he'd been shot, he'd decided it would be best, at least for now, to keep his occupation to himself while he looked into what the hell was going on at the Broken Arrow. He didn't want the neighboring ranchers or the good citizens of Willow Bend to guess what he did for a living, so he'd made the trip to Colorado with the excuse that he wanted to check on his half brother before taking the fictional job in California.

Guilt pulled at him at the thought of deceiving his brother, but he knew John would understand. And over the course of the two weeks he'd been there, things had been extremely quiet. He didn't expect that to last for long. Trouble never did. He'd learned that years ago, when he'd first worked in military intelligence, then for the CIA. He'd still be working for "the company" if it hadn't been for Sheila.

His jaw tightened at the thought of his ex-girlfriend. Beautiful, smart, fearless, she was everything he'd wanted in a woman...or so he'd thought. In reality, she was a Cuban spy. When he became suspicious of her, she fled the U.S., but not without first warning him that he would pay for destroying her cover.

Two weeks later, a sniper took a shot at him from a bridge in Virginia. The police claimed it was just a random act of violence, but he knew better. Disillusioned, he quit, changed his name and disappeared for awhile. When he finally settled down, he chose a town in Texas that was so small that everyone literally knew everyone else. No one, he'd promised himself, who wanted to harm him or his family would ever be able to sneak into his life again without him knowing about it.

And since John was engaged to Elizabeth, that made her—and the rest of the Wyatts—family. He intended to watch over all of them and find out who the hell was trying to drive them away. He didn't believe for a moment that it would be easy. He didn't know the people of Willow Bend, didn't know the dynamics of the place or which of the local citizens thought they'd been robbed of the Broken Arrow by Hilda Wyatt's will. Who was desperate enough to attack the ranch? Who wouldn't blink twice at blowing up the old Spanish gold mine or burning the cabin where John and Elizabeth planned to live? Who shot his brother?

He would find out, he vowed silently. He'd have to keep a low profile, though. As long as everyone thought he was a flirt and a tease, just killing time until his new job started, no one suspected his real reason for being there. He intended to keep it that way.

The minute dinner was over, Katherine helped Elizabeth and Rainey with the dishes as she waited for Buck to finish his evening work on the computer in his office. She hadn't bothered to bring her laptop with her because of the difference in electrical outlets, so she had no choice but to sign up for online dating on the ranch computer.

Just the thought of that brought the sting of a blush to her cheeks. She knew it was crazy, but she hated to look for a man online in front of her entire family. It was like…kissing a beau in front of her father. She shouldn't have been self-conscious—after all, she was twenty-eight years old, for heaven's sake. She wasn't doing anything illegal or immoral, and she certainly had nothing to be embarrassed about.

So why did she feel like a sixteen-year-old sneaking out to meet her boyfriend?

"Well, if it isn't Miss Five-Foot-Two-Looking-For-Mr.-Lonely," Hunter suddenly said from behind her. "What are you doing skulking in the back hall? I thought you'd already be scouting out the loser hunks on the Internet."

Startled, she whirled to find Hunter surveying her in amusement. "Do you have radar where I'm concerned or something?" she snapped. "Every time I turn around, you're right behind me. If I didn't know better, I'd swear you were following me."

"It's those big blue eyes of yours," he teased. "I just can't resist you when you bat them at me."

"When I *what?*" she gasped, outraged. "I don't do anything of the kind!"

"And then there's that come-hither smile of yours," he continued with a broad grin. "I'm telling you, if you put a picture on the Internet that captures your eyes and smile, you're going to be beating men off with a stick by the end of the week."

"The only man I'm going to be beating is you," she retorted, glaring at him. "Don't you have something else to do?"

"You mean other than tease you?" he chuckled. "Are you kidding? What could be more fun than that?"

"Breathing," she said promptly. "If you don't stop pestering me—"

The door to Buck's office opened then, and he stepped out, his sharp gaze quickly taking in the temper sparking in her eyes and Hunter's wide grin. "Uh-oh. Looks like the fur's about to fly. Better watch yourself, Hunter. The last time I saw that look in her eye, I thought she was going to pull out every hair in my head. And all just because I borrowed her bicycle without asking her."

"You didn't just borrow it—you brought it back with a flat tire," she told him, fighting a reluctant smile. "And I didn't lay a hand on that precious hair of yours. Though I should have," she added, frowning at him. "You never did pay me for that tire."

"Send me a bill," he chuckled. "So what did Hunter do to set you off?"

"Nothing," he said with an easy grin before she could open her mouth. "She's just a little huffy because she thinks I'm following her. All I was doing was going to the kitchen for a snack."

"Really?" she sniffed. "You're hungry? We just finished dinner an hour ago."

"I didn't eat much," he retorted. "I couldn't take my eyes off you."

"Oh, please!"

Laughing, Buck stepped around them. "I'm out of here."

"Buck, wait!"

"Can't," he said. "Rainey and I are going to watch a movie."

He was gone before she could stop him, leaving her alone with Hunter. "Looks like it's just you and me, kid," he drawled. "C'mon, let's go check out the Internet and see what kind of online dating services are out there."

"You must be joking."

At her dry comment, he swallowed a laugh. Damn, he liked her! She was just so easy to tease. Did she have a clue how cute she was when she looked down her nose at him that way? Maybe he should ask her out and save her the trouble of joining a dating service. They could have a lot of fun together.

Even as the appealing thought tugged at him, he stiffened. No, dammit, he wasn't going there. After Sheila had betrayed him the way she had, he'd sworn he would never trust a woman again. And in the five years that had passed since Sheila had tried to have him killed, he hadn't once been tempted to break that promise to himself.

That didn't mean he'd turned into a hermit. He liked women, enjoyed their company, not to mention sex. And finding a date wasn't a problem. He just made sure that the women he took out were just as disillusioned as he was and wanted nothing to do with a ring on their fingers. Even then, he didn't date any woman more than twice. He didn't intend to ever again give a woman a chance to get close enough to betray him.

"What?" he asked innocently. "You don't trust me?"

"Not as far as I can throw you," she retorted sweetly. "Now, if you'll excuse me, I have a date with a computer."

Without a word, she turned and walked into Buck's office, but if she thought he was so easily discouraged, she was in for a rude awakening. When she took a seat in front of the computer on Buck's desk, he followed her and pulled a chair beside her before she even knew what he was about.

"Hunter—"

"I can help you with your profile," he said at her warning tone. Thanks to his years in intelligence, he was damn good at sizing up a person, though he had no intention of telling her how he'd come by that kind of experience. "C'mon, Kitty-Kat, lighten up. If you want to get a good match, you want to word this thing just right. I can give you a man's perspective."

"I'm sure you will," she said dryly. "Thanks, but no, thanks."

"How are you going to describe yourself?"

"That's none of your business."

"Let me guess," he said, eyeing her speculatively. "You'll probably say you're cute, outgoing, artistic, with weight proportionate to your height." When her blue eyes widened in surprise, he grinned mockingly. "Am I right or what?"

"So what if you are?" she tossed back. "What's wrong with that?"

"You're writing for a man, remember?" he pointed

out. "Cute means ordinary, outgoing likes to hog the conversation."

"That's not true!"

"Artistic means you have one of those old houses that's decorated with lace and fru-fru flowery stuff. And weight proportionate to height can mean only one thing. You're fat."

"I am not!"

"Of course you're not. But that's what any man who reads that description is going to think. And that's okay if you don't care that the only men who answer your ad are losers who still live with their mothers and wear their pants up to their armpits. Of course, if that's what you want..."

Horrified, she cringed. "No, of course not."

"Then you're going to have to write a hell of a better description than that."

She should have told him no. From the glint in his eye, he was enjoying himself far too much, and for all she knew, he was just pulling her leg. But what if he wasn't kidding? If she was really going to join a dating service, the last thing she wanted was to attract one of those lonely, nerdy men who'd never had a woman in his life and wouldn't know what to do with one if he did.

"All right," she sighed. "If you're really serious about helping me...but no funny business! Understood?"

"Yes, ma'am," he replied obediently, his grin wide. "Whatever you say, ma'am."

He did, of course, do nothing but tease and torment her for the course of the next hour, and she couldn't help but laugh. When they were finished, however, she had to admit that her profile sounded far better than something she would have written herself. Still, she wasn't sure.

"It sounds like I'm tooting my own horn," she said, frowning. "Maybe we should tone some of this down."

"Are you kidding? Like what?"

"Well, like…'adventuresome'…"

"Didn't you go off to Scotland by yourself when you found out that jerk you were in love with was married? Didn't you jump on a plane and head for Colorado without even letting your family know you were coming until you were almost here?"

"Well, yes, but—" Frowning, she studied the words on the computer screen that made her sound like a fascinating catch that any man with any brains in his head would love to be matched with. "Maybe we shouldn't include the bit about me being an award-winning illustrator."

"But you are, aren't you?" When she had to agree, he said, "You're just telling the truth. And don't think for one minute that I'm going to let you take out the part about pretty. This isn't the time for hiding your light under a bushel. You are pretty, and if it was left up to me, I'd say you were downright gorgeous—"

"You're flirting again," she scolded. "You've got to stop that."

"No, I'm not," he retorted, and there was no question that he was dead serious. "You're gorgeous, but I know you won't go for that, so we have to go with pretty. That's okay. Because when you finally let your matches see your picture, they're going to know the truth, anyway."

She didn't consider herself gorgeous by any stretch

of the imagination—that word was reserved for movie stars and beauty pageant queens—but she couldn't deny that she was flattered. If he hadn't been such a flirt, she might have believed he was sincere.

"Okay, so it's settled. We leave it as it is." And without giving her a chance to argue further, he reached over and hit the enter button on the keyboard. And there, for all her prospective matches to read, was a description of her that sounded amazing.

If you're looking for a fascinating, fun-loving, adventuresome woman to spend the rest of your life with, you've found her. I'm a pretty brunette with expressive blue eyes, enticing smile and great figure, who loves pillow talk, dancing, intimate dinners for two, spontaneous, romantic trips to the mountains and holding hands. I'm a fantastic cook, award-winning illustrator, honest, sincere and looking for Mr. Right. If you think you could be him, I'd love to hear from you.

Thanks to Hunter's help, she didn't doubt that she would get any number of answers to her profile. The question was...how many of them would be like Nigel?

Katherine had heard about women who signed up with an online dating service, then became so obsessed with it that they checked their computers every day, sometimes two or three times a day. She'd sworn she wasn't going to do that, but less than twenty-four hours later, she found herself back at the computer, typing in her password to Love-n-Marriage.com.

"I thought I'd catch you here."

Startled, she glanced sharply over her shoulder to see Hunter standing in the doorway, grinning at her. "I thought you'd gone into town to get fencing material," she said with a frown.

"Buck left a list of some things he wanted me to pick up for him," he told her as he strolled into the ranch office. "It's supposed to be on his desk." Glancing at the computer screen, he arched a dark brow at her. "So how's it coming? Find Mr. Right yet?"

"I haven't even looked," she said loftily. "I was just checking my e-mails."

Wicked laughter danced in his eyes. "Oh, yeah? Then how come your matches just popped up on the screen?"

He had her and they both knew it. Cursing the heat in her cheeks, she shrugged. "I guess I punched the wrong keys."

"I guess so," he retorted with a grin. Glancing at the screen, he whistled softly. "Looks like you've got a lot of matches." When she just looked at him, he chuckled. "I guess you'd rather read them in private."

"That was the plan," she said dryly.

"I understand. No problem. Just give me a few seconds and I'll be out of your hair."

As promised, he found Buck's list almost immediately, but he didn't excuse himself and leave her alone as Katherine had expected. Instead, before she could guess his intentions, he covered her hand with his on the mouse, moved the curser and clicked.

"Hunter! Stop that! What do you think you're doing?"

"Checking these dudes out," he said promptly, nodding at the list of matches on the screen. Lightning quick, he clicked the mouse again and brought up the picture of the first man on the list.

"Ouch! He's not Brad Pitt, is he? Or Tom Hanks, for that matter. Not that there's anything wrong with Tom Hanks. He's a hell of an actor and seems like a genuinely nice guy. I guess you women would call him cute, but man, this guy is homely! What's he do for a living? He makes toys! Yeah, I'll bet he does."

"Hunter!"

"Oh, my God!" Quickly reading the man's profile, he growled, "Just like I thought. The dude's bad news."

"Just because he makes toys—"

"He knits—"

"There's nothing wrong with that—"

"—*and* collects medieval weapons," he finished with a scowl. "Think about it. A toymaker who collects medieval weapons? What's wrong with this picture? He sounds like a nutcase!"

"You don't know that. You don't know anything about him."

"I know as much as you do," he pointed out. "What do you think he's looking for? I bet it's someone who's sweet and kind and just wants to be a wife and mother."

"You don't know that," she began, only to blink when she read more of the toymaker's profile. Hunter had quoted him almost word for word. "How did you know?" she asked, surprised.

"It's easy enough to figure out," he said simply. "He probably thinks that someone whose only ambition is to be a wife and mother wouldn't be sharp enough to realize he's got a problem. What planet is he living on?"

"You don't know that he has a problem—"

"Sweetheart, I'd bet the ranch on it. And looky here,"

he taunted, checking the computer screen again. "He wants to start communications with you. He must think you could be the woman he's looking for."

Heat singeing her cheeks, she closed the file with a single click. "Whatever he thinks is none of your business."

"The hell it isn't. If you're foolish enough to go out with this jackass, I'll probably be the one who has to rescue your pretty little butt. I'm just trying to save myself some work."

She arched a delicate brow. "Excuse me, but I don't remember asking you to rescue me from anything. I can take care of myself."

"I've never met a woman yet who didn't think that. Everyone needs help once in a while, Katherine."

"I know," she said stiffly. "But I've already made a fool of myself over one man. I'm not going to do it again."

"No one plans to make a mistake," he pointed out quietly. "If you need help, you know where I am." Leaving her to her matches, he headed for the door. "Tell MW I said hello."

Confused, she frowned. "MW?"

"Medieval weapon," he retorted with a grin and walked out.

Frowning, she stared at the picture of the man on the screen. Just because he liked antique weapons didn't mean he had a problem. The least she could do was give him a chance.

The decision made, she opened the file to communicate, answered all his questions, then wrote a few questions of her own. The second she hit the send key, however, doubts tugged at her. What was she doing?

Was Hunter right? MW's info didn't add up. What if he was some kind of weirdo? Did she really want to risk communicating with someone like that?

Giving in to instinct, she moved the cursor and canceled the match.

Chapter 4

"So…how's MW?"

In the process of sitting down to breakfast with the family three mornings later, Katherine frowned in confusion. "I beg your pardon?"

"Medieval weapon," he reminded her with an arch of a brow. "Has he asked you out yet?"

Aware of the fact that the entire family was waiting expectantly for her answer, she reluctantly said, "No. I decided to…cancel him."

The last two words came out in a rush—she hoped he would let them slide by without a comment, but she should have known better. A crooked grin propped up one corner of his mouth. "No kidding? Why?"

She shrugged. "I didn't think we were suited."

"Why?"

"Because we weren't," she retorted, glaring at him in irritation. "Anyway, I found someone else I like better. I'm meeting him for lunch Friday afternoon."

That got the rest of the family's attention. "What?" Elizabeth said excitedly. "You have a date?"

"Who is he?" Buck asked with a frown. "What do you know about him?"

This was the last thing she wanted—a grilling by the family about something that should have been nothing more than an ordinary blind date. But she knew they weren't going to drop the subject until she gave them some details. "He's a rancher. He lives about a hundred miles south of Willow Bend."

"And?"

At Buck's arch, expectant look, she added, "And he's divorced. His ex-wife was a teacher. He thought they had a good marriage until he caught his wife playing around with one of her students."

"Oh, no!" Rainey exclaimed, grimacing in distaste. "Was she arrested?"

"She's in jail right now. He divorced her last summer."

"And he's a rancher?" John said with a frown. "What's his name?"

"Kurt Russell."

"Kurt Russell?" Buck said, surprised. "The movie star? I thought he was with Goldie Hawn."

"Not *that* Kurt Russell. He says he gets a lot of kidding about that. He was named after his grandfather."

"What's the name of his ranch?" John asked.

"I don't know. He didn't say."

Not liking the sound of that, Buck said, "When I joined the Cattleman's Association, I checked out the state membership, just in case I needed to call on someone for advice. I don't remember reading about anyone by the name of Kurt Russell."

"Maybe he's not a member," Katherine pointed out. "It's not a requirement, is it?"

"No, of course not. I just wish we knew a little more about this chap before you went out with him."

"I'm not going out with him," she replied. "I'm meeting him for lunch. There's a difference."

"Oh, sure," Hunter drawled. "What difference will that make when you're alone with the man fifty miles from home. He could drug you—"

"We're meeting at the Rusty Bucket," she retorted, just barely resisting the urge to throw a *Na-nanna-na-na* at him. "We may not have a lot of friends in Willow Bend, but Kurt doesn't know that. He'd be an idiot to try anything in a restaurant full of locals, right in the middle of lunch. It's the best restaurant in town, isn't it? I'll bet the sheriff or one of his deputies eats lunch there just about every day."

"She's got you there, guys," Rainey chuckled. "Back off. She'll be fine."

"Do you even know what he looks like?" Hunter asked Katherine. "How are you going to know this bozo?"

Insulted, she stiffened. "He's not a clown. And for your information, he sent me a picture. He's very nice looking."

"If he sent you *his* picture," he retorted. "For all you know, the one he sent could have been cut out of a magazine."

"And what would be the point of that?" she demanded. "The second he introduced himself, I would know he'd sent the wrong picture."

"True," he agreed. "But he may have no intention of actually talking to you. It just depends on what his agenda is. If he's some kind of creep, he could size you up from across the restaurant without you even knowing it, then follow you home to find out where you live. Or, if you measure up to his expectation, he'll approach you, apologize for sending the wrong picture, and claim that he was nervous that *he* wouldn't measure up. And you'll forgive him for misleading you from the word go."

"You think I'm that easy?"

The second the words left her tongue, she knew she'd made a mistake. A wicked grin curled the corners of his mouth. "Only you can answer that."

Oh, he thought he was clever. Her gaze locked with his, but from the corner of her eye, she could see the rest of the family biting back smiles. Silently cursing the color burning her cheeks, she lifted her chin. "I'm not going to answer that. You're going to think what you want, anyway."

"Probably."

"But just for the sake of discussion, let's say that Kurt did send me a different picture so that I wouldn't know who he was while he sums me up. What do you think he's going to do if I don't measure up?"

"You must be joking."

"It could happen."

"Never in a million years, sweetheart. Take a look in the mirror."

Her eyes narrowed suspiciously. "Are you flirting with me?"

He grinned. "What was your first clue? Your date

will, too. And he'll try to get in your panties the first chance he gets, too, so be careful. He could have all kinds of diseases."

"Hunter! Stop that."

At Rainey's quickly muffled, laughing protest, he shrugged without apology. "Hey, it's a blind date—an Internet date. He wouldn't be surfing the Web for a woman unless he had something to hide."

"You don't know anything about him," Katherine snapped, stung. "He was very sincere—"

"You spoke to him?"

Why did he always know just the right question to ask to win his point? she wondered in annoyance. "No, I haven't spoken to him," she said through her teeth. "I was referring to his e-mails."

"Which may or may not be anything more than pure fiction," he retorted. "Don't believe a word any man says until you see the whites of his eyes, and even then, take everything with a grain of salt."

"Not everyone's as cynical as you are," she returned coolly. "I prefer to take people at their word until they give me a reason not to trust them."

"Oh, God," he groaned. "You're one of those!"

"One of what?"

"One of those people who walk around with their heads in the clouds, thinking everyone's sweet and kind and nothing bad is ever going to happen to anyone. People like you need a keeper."

"Well, it won't be you."

"Don't knock it until you've tried it, sweetheart," he drawled, winking at her. "I can think of several women who enjoyed being kept by me."

Elizabeth just barely choked back a laugh—Buck and John didn't even try to stifle their chuckles. To her credit, Rainey, at least, tried to frown at Hunter. If a smile tugged at the corners of her mouth, there didn't seem to be anything she could do about it. "Hunter, that really is too much information."

"Sorry," he said, grinning.

He didn't sound the least bit sorry, but Katherine had no intention of continuing the discussion further. "Don't stop on my account," she said stiffly, pushing back her chair. "I've got better things to do."

She didn't miss the pointed looks the three men exchanged—she might be leaving, but the questions about Kurt Russell were far from over. Why were they blowing a blind date into such a big thing? she wondered, frowning. She was meeting the man in a very public place and had no intention of being alone with him. If she didn't like him—or was bored out of her mind—she could always say she wasn't feeling well or had forgotten an appointment and needed to leave. Unless the man was a complete Neanderthal, he would graciously accept the excuse and that would be that.

So what was everyone so worried about?

Friday morning dawned cool and wet. Staring out at the gray day, Katherine had little enthusiasm for her lunch date with Kurt. She'd tossed and turned all night, and as much as she wanted to attribute that to nerves over her first blind date in years, she knew it was all Hunter's fault. For the past three days, he'd done nothing but needle her about her upcoming date. He'd blatantly admitted he'd done an Internet search of Kurt Russell, but he'd discovered nothing. As far as Hunter was concerned, that made Kurt all the more suspicious.

Irritated, Katherine had tried defending Kurt. Just because he wasn't on the Internet didn't mean anything. Maybe he was new to the area. Maybe he really did use a fictitious name—not because he had something to hide but because *he* needed to protect himself from any nutcase women he might meet online. After all, women weren't the only ones who were vulnerable.

Hunter had snorted at that. Any man who couldn't protect himself from a woman was a wuss. If Kurt Russell was that weak, she didn't need him anyway.

Standing in front of her open bedroom closet, trying to decide what to wear, Katherine frowned. Why did she put any stock in what Hunter said? Just because he was John's brother didn't mean he knew what he was talking about. Especially when it came to Kurt, she reminded herself. He'd never read any of Kurt's e-mails, had no idea how kind and considerate he was.

He was wrong about him, Katherine assured herself. If her stomach was in knots at the thought of meeting Kurt, it wasn't because she didn't trust him. She just hated blind dates. After the initial first awkward moment, when he hesitated, not sure if he should kiss her on the cheek or not, they would both settle down and everything would be fine.

And it wasn't as if he was asking her to marry him or anything, she reminded herself as she pulled a red skirt and a white tank top from the closet. They were just having lunch, nothing more. It really was no big deal.

Satisfied she had everything under control, she stood

before the antique cheval mirror in her bedroom and studied herself critically. Feminine, but not too revealing, she decided. She looked nice. Now, it was time to find out if Kurt was.

Over the course of the past few weeks, she'd been practicing driving stick shift with Buck. She'd driven all over the Broken Arrow, including out to the cabin, without ever leaving the ranch. She was quite proud of her progress. She hadn't actually driven on the road by herself. Because of that, Buck had volunteered to drive her to the Rusty Bucket, then come back for her later. But she'd cringed just at the idea of being driven to her date like a nine-year-old being dropped off at school, and insisted on driving herself, instead.

And she did all right. If her heart pounded crazily and her fingers were far from steady, she told herself it had nothing to do with her upcoming blind date and everything to do with the fact that she was driving by herself for the first time on an American road. Then she carefully pulled into the parking lot of the Rusty Bucket and turned into a space between two huge, dusty pickup trucks. Just that easily, she knew she'd only been lying to herself. Her heart turned over just at the thought of meeting Kurt Russell.

Was he there?

Glancing around the full parking lot, she wanted to kick herself for not asking him what he'd be driving. He was a rancher, but that didn't mean he'd come in a pickup. For all she knew, the red Lexus convertible parked in the corner could be his.

So go inside and look for the man, a voice drawled in her head. *He's waiting for you.*

He probably was, and that sent her stomach into a nosedive. Too late she realized she might not be ready to jump back into the dating scene, after all. Especially online dating. She'd never done it before, but her friends had, and they'd had nothing good to say about it. She'd heard the horror stories, heard about the men who described themselves as tall, dark and handsome who turned out to be short, balding and attractive in a way that only a mother could love. What was she doing?

Gnawing her bottom lip, she hesitated at the entrance to the Rusty Bucket. What if Hunter was right? What if Kurt Russell had lied about his profile? What if he was an ax murderer or something?

Suddenly realizing she was actually considering Hunter's opinion seriously, she stiffened. It didn't matter if her date lied about his profile, if he was short and fat or thirty years older than he claimed. It didn't even matter if he was the loser Hunter predicted he was. She wasn't really looking for a man. All she wanted was to get her feet wet dating again…and to find someone who could take her mind off Hunter until he left for his new job in California.

Relieved that she had everything worked out in her mind, she checked her makeup in the rearview mirror, renewed her lipstick and smiled at herself in the mirror. "You're not looking for Mr. Wonderful," she told her reflection in the mirror, "so chill out. You're just going to lunch. Enjoy yourself."

That was easier said than done. Thousands of butterflies flocked in her stomach as she walked into the Rusty Bucket. Kurt had told her that he would be waiting for her at the bar and she wouldn't be able to miss him—he'd be wearing a red shirt and jeans. At least finding him wouldn't be difficult.

Four cowboys sat at the bar, however. And all four wore jeans…and shirts that could be classified as red—thin red stripes, red plaid, red checked, wide red stripes.

Stunned, Katherine stopped dead in her tracks and just barely swallowed a groan. This could not be happening!

For all of ten seconds, she gave serious consideration to turning around and walking out. God, she hated blind dates! And for just this reason. She felt like a fool, standing there, studying four different men from the rear. What if they turned and caught her staring? Heat climbed in her cheeks just at the thought.

"Katherine?"

Lost in her thoughts, she stiffened as one of the four cowboys suddenly turned and spied her standing just inside the door, staring at him and the other men at the bar. Dressed in a red-checked shirt and pressed jeans, he turned back to retrieve something from the bar, then started toward her with a smile. In a single glance, she saw that he wasn't the loser that Hunter had described, but quite attractive, though in a baby-faced kind of way. Not that there was anything wrong with that, she assured herself as she took in his black curly hair, a quick smile and dimples. Lots of women were quite taken with boyish good looks. Just because she wasn't didn't mean anything. She wasn't looking for a man, just a distraction.

"I'm Kurt," he said with an easy smile and held out a rose to her. "It's nice to finally meet you."

"Oh!" Touched, she took the flower, appreciating the gesture, but not fooled by it. He might appear boyish and charming, but she hadn't missed the quick flash of confidence in his pale blue eyes. "You didn't have to do that, but thank you. It's beautiful."

"Not as beautiful as you."

The line was so pat and outrageous, she burst out laughing. "Really? Does that line work for you often?"

"Not often enough." He chuckled. His smile rueful, he held out his hand. "Shall we start over? I'm Kurt Russell. And you're Katherine. You're prettier than your picture."

Charmed in spite of herself, she smiled. "I bet you say that to all your dates."

"Just the pretty ones," he assured her with a laugh.

Not believing him for a second, she grinned. "There you go again with another line."

"I'm serious!"

"You really don't have to try so hard," she said dryly. "I'm not looking for a husband or significant other or someone to father the children I will probably have one day. Right now, I'm just looking for a friend."

His grin faded, his eyes searched hers, and he obviously found what he was looking for there. "You've found one," he said simply. "C'mon. Let's get a table. I want to know everything about you."

Flattered, she let him lead her to a table by the window and was soon thoroughly enjoying herself. She hadn't planned to let herself like Kurt. Not yet, anyway, she amended. But he was funny and charming and, in spite of the baby face, very attractive. Within ten minutes of sitting down across the table from him, she knew she would say yes if he asked her out again.

Shocked by the sudden direction of her thoughts, she looked quickly away. Had she lost her mind? What was she thinking—

Her gaze collided with mocking green eyes, but it was a full ten seconds before she blinked into focus the man seated across the restaurant from where she and Kurt sat. Hunter! Even in the intimate lighting of the Rusty Bucket, she would have recognized him anywhere. And he was watching her and Kurt's every move.

He'd followed her!

Just that quickly she was livid. How dare he! He'd followed her like an overprotective father, then retreated to the shadows to watch in case he was needed. Furious, she couldn't believe his audacity. She hadn't asked for his help, didn't want it. She wasn't a fourteen-year-old who'd never been out of the house alone after dark, for heaven's sake. She didn't need him to protect her, look out for her, babysit her. And she was going to damn well tell him that!

"Hey, where you going?"

Halfway out of her chair, she only just then remembered Kurt. Heat stung her cheeks. "I'm sorry. I just noticed my sister's brother-in-law—"

"The guy by the bar?" he said easily.

Oh, God, he'd noticed Hunter watching, she thought, mortified as she fought the need to look Hunter's way again. "Actually, he's not Elizabeth's brother-in-law yet, but he's staying at the ranch until he starts a new job next month. I didn't expect him to be here."

"Would you like to ask him to join us?"

"Oh, God, no!"

He laughed at her horrified tone. "Why do I have the feeling that you don't like him very much?"

"He likes pushing my buttons," she said flatly.

"So why's he here? Is he following you? Or just checking me out?"

"I have no idea," she retorted. "I prefer not to think about him if I don't have to."

"Then we won't," he said easily. "I'd much rather talk about you. What in the world is a woman like you doing looking for a man on the Internet?"

"I could ask you the same thing," she said, grinning. "You don't need me to tell you how good-looking you are. What are you doing on the Internet?"

His eyes twinkled merrily. "Looking for you, of course. So...what would you like for lunch? I'm going to have a steak."

"I'll call you," Kurt promised an hour and a half later as he walked her to her car and kissed her on the cheek. "Maybe we can go out to dinner and a movie next week."

"I'd love that," she said with a smile. "So I guess I'll talk to you in a couple of days."

"Sounds good. Take care. I really enjoyed myself."

Tracing a teasing finger down her nose, he headed for his car across the parking lot, then waved as he drove away. Watching him, Katherine had to admit that she'd thoroughly enjoyed lunch. It was, in fact, the best blind date she'd ever had. Who knew Internet dating could be so much fun?

She hadn't, however, forgotten about Hunter. Turning on her heel, she marched back into the restaurant. Irritating man. So he thought he could spy on her, did he? They'd just see about that!

"I want to talk to you," she said as she reached his table. "How dare you!"

"How dare I?" he taunted, making no effort to hide his amusement. "What did I do? I just came in here for a nice leisurely lunch, and what do I find? You falling for some Romeo's line of bull. You disappoint me, Kitty-Kat. I didn't think you were that naive."

Her eyes snapped fire at that. "For your information, I haven't fallen for anyone, but even if I have, what business is that of yours? And don't pretend for a second that you just wandered in here by chance. You're following me!"

He didn't even try to deny it. "I thought you might need me," he said simply. "Obviously, I was right. You gave him your phone number, didn't you?"

Irritated, she couldn't deny it. "So? What's that got to do with you?"

"Nothing," he said with a shrug. So why did watching her with Mr. Wonderful twist his guts in a knot? Annoyed with the direction of his thoughts, he added, "It isn't me I'm concerned about. I'm not the one who coughed up my phone number to a jerk I don't know anything about just because he made me laugh."

"I know enough. He told me—"

"What he wanted you to know, silly," he cut in. "And you bought it. What were you thinking? That just because he was funny and reasonably attractive, he was safe? What was the harm? C'mon, you're smarter than that."

When he said it like that, she wanted to sink right through the floor. She *was* smarter than that. She wasn't even interested in dating anyone, but Kurt had seemed nice and, just as Hunter said, safe. And, she realized too late, he could have been lying through his teeth the entire time. Hadn't Nigel? God, when was she going to learn?

"I hate it when you're right," she retorted.

"It's not so bad when you get used to it." He chuckled. "And it's not my fault you need a keeper. I'm just trying to help out."

"Oh, really?" she said archly. "And you think you're the man for the job?"

"You're damn straight," he said promptly. And with nothing more than a flash of his wicked grin to warn her he was up to mischief, he reached for her and pulled her into his arms. She only had time to gasp before his mouth covered hers.

Chapter 5

Her blood roaring in her ears, her heart pounding, Katherine swayed as he finally let her up for air and set her from him. All around them, other diners broke into wide grins, hoots and hollers and scattered applause. Later, she knew she would be mortified, but for now, all she wanted to do was step back into his arms.

And Hunter knew that—she could see it in his eyes. Lightning quick, she was so mad she could have spit fire. Uncaring that dozens of other patrons were watching their every move, she snapped, "What the devil do you think you're doing?"

"Showing you how a real man kisses a woman goodbye," he retorted with a grin. "Do I have to teach you everything? You should know this stuff by now."

Fuming, Katherine didn't know if she wanted to slap

that grin off his face or string him up by his thumbs. He didn't give her a chance to do either. Winking at her, he said, "See you around, sweetheart," and strolled out of the Rusty Bucket as if he didn't have a care in the world.

Frustrated, Katherine snatched up a napkin from the table and threw it after him. All around her, people chuckled.

Thirty minutes later Kurt Russell, aka Elliot Fletcher, arrived at his apartment in Red Bluff, Colorado, and smiled in satisfaction at the thought of Katherine. She was going to do nicely. She'd bought his story, lock, stock and barrel, and didn't suspect for a second that everything he'd told her had been nothing but a lie. There was no ranch—far from it, in fact, he thought bitterly. He lived in a dump of an apartment that should have been condemned years ago, and he was too damned good for it. And then there was his bitch of an ex-wife. She wasn't in jail, though he wouldn't lose any sleep over her if she was. She'd never been a teacher—never even finished high school—and she wouldn't have had the nerve to play around on him. The one time she'd been stupid enough to look at another man, he'd beat the hell out of her. She'd never done it again, not while they were married, and not after he'd divorced her lazy ass. He didn't share his women, even when he didn't want them anymore.

Katherine would learn that soon enough. Once he'd charmed her into his bed, she sure as hell wouldn't be looking at another man the way she had her sister's brother-in-law at the Rusty Bucket. He'd make sure of it. She'd know her place and stay there.

But first, he had to win her trust. He'd do it, he thought confidently. She was pretty, recovering from a broken heart and, better yet, she didn't have a clue that he had a long history of duping women out of money. He'd take his time with her, woo her and get everything he could out of her.

The question was...what did she really have? He knew her family owned a ranch, but she was playing her cards close to her vest. She hadn't told him her last name or the name of her family ranch, but she'd said enough for him to know it was thousands of acres. And that meant money. Now it was just a question of getting his hands on as much of it as possible.

A sinister smile curled the edges of his mouth as he contemplated just how much money the lovely Katherine might have. She dressed well, had great manners and gave every appearance of being born with a silver spoon in her mouth. That might be because of her very proper British accent, but he didn't think so. The lady had class written all over her, and if he played his cards right, he might just hit the jackpot.

When the phone on his computer desk rang, he didn't have to check his caller ID to know that the caller wasn't Katherine. He'd given her his cell phone number, not the landline. So who the hell was calling? Only a handful of people had his number, but he usually insisted on calling them.

Frowning at the caller ID, which only showed PRIVATE NAME/PRIVATE NUMBER, he hesitated. Had one of his friends gotten a new phone? He should let the machine answer it, but he didn't know anyone who was stupid enough to leave a message. Messages were…evidence. A smart man didn't leave them.

Making a snap decision, he snatched up the phone. "Who is this?"

If Katherine had heard the cold snarl that came out of his mouth, she would have been not only shocked, but intimidated. The caller was neither. "This is your new best friend, Mr. Fletcher," an obviously disguised voice said mockingly. "How would you like to make ten grand?"

His blood ran cold. Fletcher. The jackass, whoever he was, knew his real name. "That depends," he said coolly. "What do I have to do?"

"You had a lunch date with Katherine Wyatt today. Are you familiar with her family and the Broken Arrow Ranch?"

Stunned, Elliot blinked. She was a *Wyatt?* The ones from England who stood to inherit one of the largest ranches in Colorado if they could manage to stay there for a year without being absent two nights in a row? Of course he'd heard of them.

"Everyone in Colorado knows about the Wyatts and the Broken Arrow Ranch," he said. "What's that got to do with me?"

"More than you know," the caller retorted. "Do whatever you have to to convince the Wyatts to leave the Broken Arrow for two nights in a row, and the ten thousand dollars is yours."

"And how do you propose I do that? From what I've heard, they're a hell of a lot more persistent than most people thought they would be."

"They're thieves," the caller said in an icy, mechanical

voice that could have been either male or female. "They have no right to the land. They're not even Americans!"

"I didn't know that was a prerequisite for owning land in the United States," Elliot said dryly.

"It's not!" his "new best friend" snarled, "but it should be! Do whatever you have to. Just get rid of the Wyatts."

Elliot had never had a scruple in his life and he didn't intend to start now. All he was interested in was the pay. "No problem," he said easily. "I won't bore you with the details. When do I get paid?"

"Check your mailbox tomorrow morning at seven for a down payment. You'll get the rest when the job's done."

"Wait," he cried before the caller could hang up. "How'd you get my number?"

His only answer was a short, humorless laugh, then a click.

The jackass had hung up on him. Anger sparked in his eyes. No one hung up on him! He had half a mind to call the jerk back and tell him—or her—off. But he didn't have the bastard's number, and he didn't mind admitting that that worried him. How *had* the caller gotten his number? No one in the area knew his real name, and even if they did, it wouldn't have done them any good. The phone was listed under one of his aliases, one he hadn't used in years, and less than a handful of people knew it. Had one of them sold him out to someone he didn't even know? Why? What the hell was going on? he wondered, scowling.

He didn't like surprises…or questions he couldn't answer. He was a man who survived by his wits, and he knew to trust his instincts. His gut told him the voice at the other end of the phone would cause him trouble before it was over with, and if he had any sense, he'd forget the job the caller wanted him to do and get the hell out of Dodge while he still could.

But ten grand! How the hell was he supposed to walk away from that? Money was tight. He'd taken some hits lately at the track, and ten grand would go a long way in making his life more comfortable.

And then there was the sheer pleasure of giving in to his darker side and terrorizing the Wyatts into leaving the Broken Arrow for a couple of nights. What could be more fun than that? he thought with a sinister smile.

Hunter beat Katherine home by ten minutes, but he was still in the front hall when she stormed through the door. He took one look at her and could practically see the steam pouring out her ears.

"I want to talk to you!"

Hunter just barely bit back a smile. "Sure thing, Kitty-Kat. Shoot."

"You are the lowest, rottenest, slimiest slug who ever crawled out from under a rock—"

"Katherine!"

Glancing over his shoulder to find Rainey standing in the doorway to the kitchen looking horrified, Hunter grinned. "It's okay, Rainey. Don't stop her now. She's been building up to this for weeks. Let her have her say. I have it coming."

"You bet you do," Katherine snapped, then told her sister-in-law, "He *kissed* me!"

For a moment Hunter thought Rainey was going to laugh. Her eyes bright with a flash of humor, she pressed a quick hand to her twitching lips. "Well," she choked, "that certainly explains it."

"This isn't funny, Rainey. He grabbed me right in the middle of the Rusty Bucket and kissed me! This is outrageous."

Biting her lip, Rainey didn't argue with her. Instead she said in a strangled voice, "I have to check something on the stove."

She whirled and rushed into the kitchen, and even as the door swung shut behind her, Hunter heard her laughing. Grinning, he lifted a dark brow at Katherine. "You were saying?"

"Leave me alone," she said tersely. "Do you hear me? Just leave me alone. I don't need you to watch over me. I don't need your help when it comes to men. Okay? Have I made myself clear?"

"As glass," he retorted. "I won't bother you again."

"Good," she retorted, and brushed past him to go into Buck's office. When he turned as if to follow her, she shut the door in his face.

Not the least bit offended, Hunter only chuckled. He'd leave her alone…when she was at home or in church or going shopping with her sister or sister-in-law. When she had a date with one of the losers she met online, that was another matter. Like it or not, he intended to be there, to watch over her, to come to her defense, if necessary. He'd made it his personal goal this summer to make sure she was safe. If she had a problem with that, too damn bad.

For the next three days, Katherine avoided Hunter like the plague. She saw him at meals, of course, but she made it a point to be where he wasn't as much as possible. And he knew exactly what she was doing. She saw the knowledge in his dancing eyes every time she ran into him in the dining room. Then there was that grin of his. Every time he flashed it at her, he set her teeth on edge. And he not only knew it, he delighted in driving her crazy.

And then there was the matter of that kiss. She wanted to dismiss it, to forget it, to tell herself that she'd felt absolutely nothing. But it still haunted her dreams, and the remembered taste of him stirred her senses every time he walked into the same room with her. It was maddening, frustrating, heart-stopping. How had she let him do this to her?

Seated across the table from him at dinner on Tuesday night, she felt her pulse throb as his eyes seemed to stroke her. Elizabeth and John had gone to Denver for a few days, so there were just Buck and Rainey and she and Hunter for dinner. And every time she looked up, he was looking right at her, watching her, making it impossible for her to concentrate on anything but him. She hardly tasted her food, let alone heard a word of the dinner conversation.

Troubled, needing some time to herself, she sighed in relief when the meal was finally over. Rainey volunteered to do the dishes, and Buck escaped to his office to take care of ranch paperwork. Before Katherine could blink, she found herself alone with Hunter in the dining room.

Then her cell phone rang.

Even before she checked the caller ID, she knew it had to be Kurt. Her friends in England e-mailed her, and no one but the family—and Kurt—had her American cell phone number. And she'd bet good money that Hunter knew it.

Lifting a mocking brow at her when her phone rang again, he said, "Aren't you going to answer it?"

"No," she retorted. "Whoever's calling will leave a message. I'll call them back."

"Is that lover boy?" he teased. "It is, isn't it? Go on...answer it. I know you must be dying to talk to him."

He didn't think she'd talk to Kurt while he was sitting right there, listening, she thought, irritated. Well, she'd show him! She could talk to any man she wanted, and she didn't give a damn who was listening.

"Of course I want to talk to him," she told him, and to prove it, she snapped open her flip phone and said brightly, "Hey, stranger. How are you?"

"Great," Kurt growled, "now that your lovely voice is purring in my ear. I haven't thought of anything but you for the last three days."

His tone was husky and intimate, and for some reason, he made her uncomfortable, but she didn't have time to analyze why. All she could think of was that Hunter could probably hear every word. Why had she let him goad her into answering the phone?

"That's very sweet of you," she said with forced lightness. "I've been thinking of you, too. I really did enjoy lunch the other day."

"Great. That's why I'm calling. Let's do it again."

"You want to go to lunch?"

"I thought maybe we could drive into Aspen. Have you been there yet?"

"No, but I'd love to go. I've heard it's beautiful."

"It is. So what day's good for you? Just pick a day. I'm free the rest of the week."

She hesitated, shooting Hunter a *get lost* look that any gentleman would have respected. Not surprisingly, he only leaned back in his chair as if he had no intention of going anywhere, and surveyed her in amusement. Frustrated, put on the spot, she said, "How about Wednesday?"

"Sounds good," Kurt replied, pleased. "Are you comfortable with me picking you up? If not, I can meet you somewhere...."

She hesitated, only to chide herself for being so foolish. If she didn't trust him, she had no business going to Aspen with him! "Of course you can pick me up," she told him, and gave him directions to the ranch.

When she hung up, Hunter leaned back in his chair and grinned mockingly. "So we're going out with Mr. Smooth on Wednesday. Where're we going? To lunch again or is he taking us out on a real date?"

Alarmed, she warned, "Don't even think about going there, Hunter. *We* aren't going anywhere."

"Sure we are. The golden boy asked you out. That means *we* have a date."

"*I* have a date," she retorted, "and you're not invited. Understood? I don't need a chaperone."

"You're crazy if you think you're safe with that joker. Haven't you noticed how smooth he is?"

"He's charming—"

"He's trouble," he said flatly.

"You don't even know him."

"I don't want to know him, and if you were smart, you wouldn't, either."

Irritated, she snapped, "I don't remember asking for your opinion. When I want your help, I'll ask for it. Until then, don't follow me, don't watch over me, don't do anything except leave me alone."

Not giving him a chance to say another word, she turned and walked out. Her bedroom was the only place on the ranch where she could be sure he wouldn't follow her, so she spent the next few hours working on the illustrations her publisher needed by next week. She didn't, however, get very far, and it was all Hunter's fault. She couldn't stop thinking of him, couldn't stop listening for his step in the hall as the hour grew late. His room was two doors past hers, and each night, she would hear his step in the hall long after she went to bed. She'd often wondered what he did so late at night, but she never asked. He would, no doubt, have given her some glib answer and teased her about being curious about him.

Nothing, she tried to assure herself, could have been further from the truth. But as she finally put her work away for the night and stepped over to her lingerie chest to retrieve her nightgown, she couldn't stop wondering about him. Was he divorced? Widowed? Never married? He'd really said very little about himself. What was his story? What kind of woman was he drawn to?

Suddenly realizing where her thoughts had wandered, she swore softly. No! She would not let the man tease her in the privacy of her own thoughts! He did enough of that when they were face-to-face. She was going to bed, and if she was going to dream of someone, it would be Kurt and their upcoming date.

But when she pulled open the top drawer of her

lingerie chest, she frowned in confusion. After she'd washed her laundry earlier that morning, she folded everything and put it away. Her gowns should have been neatly folded in the top drawer. Instead, she found herself looking at her bras.

"What in the world—"

Frowning, she shut the drawer and pulled open the second one, only to discover that the nightgowns she'd brought with her from England were there, instead of in the top drawer. Had she been so distracted that she hadn't noticed where she was putting her clean laundry that morning? she wondered. What had she been thinking about? Work? Kurt? Hunter? She couldn't remember, and at the moment she didn't really care. She just wanted to go to bed.

It was a cool evening and of the gowns she'd brought with her from England, only one was long-sleeved. There was, however, no sign of it.

"Okay," she said aloud, frustrated, "this is crazy."

She clearly remembered putting all her gowns in the top drawer. So how had her clothes ended up in the wrong drawers? And where the devil was her long-sleeved nightgown? She would have sworn it had been washed with her other lingerie, but maybe not.

Striding into her private bathroom, she checked the hamper…just in case. It was empty. Baffled, she went in search of Rainey and found her in the upstairs laundry room. "There you are," she told her. "Have you seen my pink gown? I did some laundry this morning and thought I washed my gown, but now I can't find it. Did I leave it in here?"

"I haven't seen it," she said, looking around. "Maybe

Elizabeth thought it was hers and took it with her. Why don't you call her?"

"Oh, no," she said with a grimace. "It's late, and I don't want to disturb her when she and John are on a trip. I've got other gowns, anyway. I'll just sleep in one of them and find the other one tomorrow. It's no big deal."

"I'll keep an eye out for it," Rainey promised.

Heading back to her room, Katherine only took time to switch her clothes back to the drawers they belonged in before changing into a gown and crawling into bed. Almost immediately exhaustion seemed to catch up with her, and her eyes closed on a sigh. Within seconds she was asleep.

She dreamed about nightgowns and shadows in the night, and when she woke the following morning, she felt as if she'd hardly slept at all. Groaning, she rolled out of bed and headed for the bathroom.

A hot shower, followed by a sudden burst of cold water, woke her up as nothing else could. Revived, she dressed in shorts, a cool cotton top and sandals, and pinned her damp curls up off her neck with a clip. She would work on the back porch this morning, she decided as she stepped over to the dresser to retrieve her cell phone and watch. There was a great view of the mountains and—

Her eyes on the small china dish her watch was nestled in, she frowned. Wasn't it on the opposite side of the dresser last night? And her jewelry box…it should have been pressed up against the mirror. That's where it was when she went to bed last night. How…

Then it hit her. She wasn't that forgetful. Someone had moved her things.

Hunter.

His name popped uncontested into her head. He had to be responsible. It was just the kind of thing he would do—slip into her room after she'd fallen asleep and move the things around on her dresser. He loved teasing her, playing with her mind.

Not only had he played with her mind, he'd had his hands in her lingerie!

Heat spilled into her cheeks just at the thought of her bras and panties and nightgowns slipping through his big, masculine hands. Her heart suddenly pounding, she could almost feel him touching her.

Shocked by the direction of her thoughts, she was instantly furious. This was outrageous! He couldn't keep doing this to her. He was driving her crazy, and by God, it was going to stop right now!

Grabbing her watch, she stormed downstairs to the breakfast room and didn't care that Buck and Rainey were there to witness the tongue-lashing that was to come. By the time she was through with Hunter, he was going to regret the day he ever laid eyes on her.

"How dare you!"

In the process of reading the paper, he looked up in surprise. "I beg your pardon?"

"You'd better do a hell of a lot more than that," she retorted, bearing down on him. "The next time you come into my room when I'm sleeping, you'd better be ready for a fight."

"What?"

"Hunter, you didn't!"

At Buck's and Rainey's shocked exclamations, he

grinned. "I wish I had, but I don't have a clue what she's talking about."

He was so sincere, Katherine almost believed him. But there was a twinkle in his eye and that maddening grin. "Nice try," she retorted, "but we both know you slipped into my room last night and rearranged the things on my dresser. Did you think I wouldn't notice or were you just trying to drive me crazy?"

"Why do I have a feeling it would be a short drive?" he quipped.

"Cute," she said witheringly. "This isn't about me, so don't try misdirecting the conversation, mister. And where's my nightgown?"

"Your nightgown!" Buck thundered.

"I thought Elizabeth had it," Rainey said, confused.

"So did I," Katherine told her. "But then when I saw how the things were rearranged on my dresser, I realized someone had moved my lingerie, too." Turning back to him, she said, "So where is it? If you have a lingerie fetish, save it for someone else. I'm not interested. I just want my nightgown back."

Another man might have been more than a little uncomfortable in the face of such accusations, but it took a heck of a lot more than the indignant hissing of a kitty cat to make him squirm. Amused, he sat back in his chair as if he didn't have a care in the world. "I don't have it, sweetheart. And I didn't touch anything on your dresser because I wasn't in your room."

"Yeah, right," she sniffed. "Do you think anyone here believes you? This is just the kind of thing you'd do."

He didn't deny it. "So? That doesn't mean I did."

"Why should I believe you?"

"Because I won't come into your bedroom until you invite me, and you haven't invited me...yet."

When she gasped indignantly, Buck bit back a smile. "Well, if that's the case, then I don't know how he could have done it, Katherine. Are you sure you're not imagining all this? Maybe Elizabeth does have your gown. Why don't you call her?"

"I don't need to call her," she retorted. "I washed my lingerie yesterday and put everything away in the proper drawers. I distinctly remember folding my clean gown and putting in away. Then last night, it wasn't there."

"So, you're mistaken," Hunter said easily.

"I am not!" she retorted. "I had it."

"So why don't you know where it is?"

He had the grin of a man who'd gotten away with murder, and he seemed quite proud of himself. "I do know where it is," she seethed. "You have it. You want to keep it? Go ahead. But if you come into my room again, be prepared for a fight. Don't say you weren't warned."

"Fair enough." He chuckled. "Now that we've got that settled, why don't you sit down and join us for breakfast? Would you like some eggs? They're great."

"Stuff it," she growled, and stalked out.

Chapter 6

Hunter had always been a light sleeper. The creaking of the house, the sigh of a rising wind outside—it took nothing more than that to wake him. So when John's dogs, Buster and Lucy, started barking two nights later from their kennel, which was behind the foreman's cabin where John and Elizabeth lived, he woke instantly.

Lying perfectly still in the darkness, hardly breathing, he listened, waiting to see if the dogs were barking at a skunk or raccoon that may have wandered close to the house in search of food or if something more threatening was approaching. Instead of subsiding, however, the dogs' barking became more insistent.

He'd been expecting this, Hunter thought grimly. After everything that had happened at the ranch over the past few months, things had been too quiet lately. Apparently, that was about to change.

Throwing off the single sheet that covered him, he pulled on his jeans and boots, then reached for the pistol he kept in the drawer of the nightstand next to the bed. John and Elizabeth had returned earlier in the day, and Hunter didn't doubt for a minute that John was already checking out what the dogs were barking at.

Soundlessly opening his door, he stepped out into the dark upstairs hallway, but he'd hardly taken a step toward the stairs when he heard a sound behind him and the hall light was switched on. Surprised, he whirled just in time to see Katherine join her brother and sister-in-law in the hall.

No woman had a right to look so damn sexy in the middle of the night, Hunter thought with a silent groan. Her hair was wild and tousled, her face free of makeup, the summer robe she wore barely belted over her long, pale yellow nightgown. Her bare toes peaked out from beneath the hem of her gown, and he couldn't take his eyes off them. Red-hot polish, he thought, swallowing a groan. One of his weaknesses. Later he would, he knew, dream about those pretty toes, but for now, he had other things to worry about.

A shotgun gripped comfortably in his right hand, Buck said sharply, "Did you hear the dogs, too?"

He nodded grimly. "It could be an animal."

"Or not," Rainey said, her face stark with worry as she hugged herself. "Buster and Lucy don't usually bark at stray animals."

"You mean you think someone's out there?" Katherine asked in alarm. "Who?"

"That's what we're going to find out," Buck said, and headed for the stairs.

John and Elizabeth were just coming in from the kitchen as they reached the entrance hall. John, like Buck, had a shotgun in his hand. "Elizabeth and I just saw lights in the cemetery."

"This could be a trap to get us out of the house," Buck said.

"Why don't you two go check out the cemetery," Hunter told him, "and I'll stand guard here."

"I think it would be better to call the sheriff," Katherine said worriedly. "Let the authorities handle the situation."

"Oh, we'll call them," Elizabeth told her, "but whoever's out there will be gone long before the sheriff can get here. We've got to handle it ourselves." Stepping over to John, she gave him a quick kiss. "Be careful."

"Have you got your cell phone?" Rainey asked Buck.

He nodded grimly. "I'll call if we need help. You do the same." Giving her a quick hug and kiss, he strode out with John right behind him.

Hunter wasted no time securing the homestead. "Okay, ladies, we're going to put the house in lockdown. Then I want everyone who knows how to shoot to grab a gun from the gun cabinet and take up a position at windows on opposite sides of the house."

He didn't have to tell Rainey or Elizabeth twice. They grabbed shotguns from the gun cabinet in Buck's office and within minutes had each staked out a window on the east and north side of the house.

Left alone with Katherine, Hunter studied her with a frown. "No one's taught you to shoot yet?"

She grimaced. "I don't like guns."

"We'll have to do something about that. Are you okay keeping an eye on the front door? If you see anyone coming, yell your guts out."

"Oh, I will," she promised. "The entire county will hear me."

"Good," he said with a quick grin. "Though, don't get too excited. Whoever was in the cemetery knows by now he's got the entire house in an uproar. If he's not long gone, he's crazier than I think he is."

The words were hardly out of his mouth when Buck and John returned, both their faces carved in identical expressions of disgust. "There wasn't so much as a footprint," John grumbled.

"Was anything disturbed?" Elizabeth asked.

"Not that we could find," Buck retorted. "We took the dogs, but whoever was there had already taken off."

Hugging herself, she shivered. "Could it have been teenagers looking for ghosts?"

"They wouldn't have driven all the way out here from town just for that," Hunter said with a frown. "It's not like the family cemetery is right on the road—it's five miles from the ranch entrance."

"Some might see that as a challenge that only increases the thrill," Rainey pointed out. "You know how teenagers are. They think they're invincible and will try just about anything."

Struck by a sudden thought, Katherine said, shocked, "Do you think that's what happened to my nightgown? Some teenagers sneaked into the house and stole it?"

"You're still looking for that gown?" Buck said, frowning. "I thought Elizabeth took it by mistake."

"I haven't seen it," Elizabeth retorted. "I thought Hunter had something to do with it."

"I don't even know what it looks like," Hunter told her. "I told her I hadn't been in her room, but she didn't believe me."

"Because you're always teasing me," Katherine said, scowling at him. "How am I supposed to know when you're serious?"

"Wait a minute," Rainey said with a frown. "If Hunter didn't take the gown and it didn't get mixed up with Elizabeth's laundry, then where is it?"

"It could be like a lost sock," John said. "You know it's somewhere in the house but you just can't find it."

"Or someone's been in the house...and my room." Shivering at the thought, Katherine hugged herself. "This is starting to scare me."

"There's no reason to be scared yet," Hunter told her. "Not until we know for sure what happened to your gown. It could be lost in the covers of your bed or it slipped behind the dryer or maybe you even set it down somewhere when you got a phone call or something. There are all sorts of possibilities."

"We'll search the house first thing in the morning," Buck said.

"And if we still don't find it?"

His expression turned grim. "Then we've got a problem."

The search was scheduled to start after breakfast the next morning, but the various family members had only just begun to straggle in when Elizabeth and Katherine rushed into the dining room, one after the other, looking more than a little agitated. In the process of pouring himself a cup of coffee, Hunter took one look at both their pale faces and frowned. "What's wrong now?"

"My watch is missing."

"My diamond earrings that Mother and Father gave me when I graduated are gone," Elizabeth said.

Stepping into the dining room just in time to hear their announcement, Buck swore. "Are you sure?"

"I'm positive," Katherine said. "Ever since my night-gown disappeared, I've been very conscientious of where I put things. Last night when I went to bed, I specifically put my watch on my nightstand and wrote in my diary where I was putting it." Slapping her diary down on the dining room table, she flipped it open to the last entry. "See. Watch on nightstand."

Reading the entry out loud, her words echoed in the silence as the entire family realized there was a very good possibility that their worst nightmare was coming true. "And it didn't get knocked off?" Rainey asked quietly. "You're sure?"

"I looked everywhere—under the nightstand and bed, even on the dresser and in the bathroom. It's gone."

"What about your earrings?" Hunter asked Elizabeth. "Where were they?"

"In my jewelry box." Stricken, she said, "I don't know how someone could have gotten into the cabin and taken them when John and I were right there. We're both light sleepers, and Buster and Lucy never made a sound."

"Yes, they did," John said grimly, joining the group. "When we saw the lights in the cemetery."

Elizabeth paled. "You think someone slipped into the cabin while you and Buck were at the cemetery?"

"It makes sense," he replied. "Think about it. The cabin was empty, you and the rest of the girls were here in the house with Hunter, guarding the place while Buck and I were gone. No one thought to keep an eye on the cabin."

"That doesn't explain my watch," Katherine pointed out. "No one could have slipped into the house when you and Buck were at the cemetery—we were all here, watching."

"Unless they found a way to get into the house after everything calmed down and we all went to bed," Hunter said grimly.

Katherine paled at his words. "My watch was on the nightstand right next to my bed. I was lying right there! Surely if someone came into my room, I would have known."

"Your watch is missing, sweetheart. If you're absolutely positive it was on your nightstand, then there's no other explanation."

"We also have to consider the possibility that the same person who took the watch was the same one who took Katherine's nightgown," Buck said flatly. "He obviously has unlimited access to the house."

"I'm calling the sheriff," Elizabeth said, and reached for the phone.

Deputy Darrell Marshall arrived twenty minutes later. He did a thorough inspection of the house and grounds, including the cemetery, and could do nothing but shake his head. "I hate like hell to tell you this," he told them as they all gathered in the family room, "but there's no evidence of a break-in, no fingerprints, nothing to indicate that anyone but the family was even here."

"Except that a watch and a pair of diamond earrings are missing," Buck pointed out dryly. "They didn't just get up and walk off by themselves."

"No, sir," the deputy agreed. "I'm not saying that. I'm just saying that I don't have a damn thing to go on. I think Mr. Sinclair is right—someone slipped into Mr. Cassidy's cabin while he and Mr. Wyatt were checking the intruder at the cemetery. I don't know how someone got in the house, though, without any of you knowing it. Is there a possibility someone left their keys in a car or there's a spare key hidden around the property that someone could have found?"

Buck swore. "Dammit to hell! The extra key was at the cemetery!"

"Who knew that?" Darrell demanded.

"No one. I hid the extra key up there when I first moved in. I knew there would be times when one of the girls would be here alone, and I wanted to make sure that a key was hidden far enough away from the house that no one would come across it accidentally."

"And no one saw you hide it there?"

"Well, obviously, someone did, but I didn't see them."

"Who takes care of the cemetery?"

"Albert's Funeral Home," he retorted, naming one of the two funeral homes in Willow Bend. "They come out once a month and take care of the graves."

Taking notes, he said, "I'll check it out. I need to

warn you that the odds of recovering the jewelry are slim. I'll check the pawnshops and Internet, but whoever took the jewelry could sell it anywhere. *If* they sell it," he pointed out. "It might just be a trophy."

"Do what you can," Buck told him. "Let us know if you find anything."

"Will do, sir," he assured him. "If anything else comes up, call us immediately."

The entire family knew there was little point in that, but they kept that thought to themselves. "Thanks for your help," Buck told him.

The second Darrell left, Hunter growled, "Well, that was a waste of time."

"Now you know what we're dealing with," Elizabeth said. "The police aren't much help."

"Which is why we have to take care of the situation ourselves," Buck added. "The first thing we've got to do is change the locks. Whoever's got that damn key isn't going to be able to use it more than once."

"While you're at it, you need to put up some security cameras," Hunter said. "I'll be more than happy to help you and John install some, if you like."

"Thanks," he said. "Good idea. Let's check out what we're going to need, then make a run to the hardware store. We need everything installed before dark."

Two hours later Buck and the women of the house were busy installing new locks while John and Hunter worked together to put security cameras around the perimeter of the homestead compound. By nightfall new locks would be in place and there would be cameras at every corner of the house. If they didn't run out of daylight, the barn and foreman's cabin would also be under surveillance. An intruder wouldn't be able to so much as step foot within fifty feet of the compound without a camera recording his every move.

Adjusting one of the cameras that overlooked the front of the house, Hunter asked, "I don't know who the hell helped themselves to Elizabeth's and Katherine's jewelry last night, but they're going to find their picture plastered on Wanted posters all over the county if they're stupid enough to show up here again. Think they'll be expecting cameras?"

"God only knows," John retorted in disgust. "Just when I think I'm getting a handle on these jackasses, they pull something that totally catches me off guard."

"Any idea of who we're dealing with?"

John shrugged. "Neighbors…someone who thinks they have a grudge against the Wyatts…any number of people who want to use Hilda's will as an excuse to break the law."

"Or all of the above," Hunter said.

"Or all of the above," his brother agreed. "That's why it's so difficult to catch anyone. The attacks are coming from a hundred different directions."

"Somebody's bound to screw up," Hunter began, only to frown as a fancy red sports car came careening down the driveway like a bat out of hell. "What the hell—"

Through narrowed eyes, he studied the driver. There was something about the man that looked vaguely familiar. Then recognition hit him. "Well, I'll be damned. I do believe that's the infamous Kurt Russell. Kat's got a date. With everything going on, I bet she forgot."

In the process of changing the lock on the front door, Buck turned to survey the new arrival and lifted a brow in surprise as Kurt stepped out of the sports car. "He's not Katherine's usual type. A little too soft."

"I don't know why she's even bothering with a second date," Hunter retorted. "He's a loser."

"Maybe it's time I checked him out." Setting his screwdriver down, Buck headed for the front drive.

"You must be Kurt," he said as he approached him with a hand outstretched in greeting. "I'm Buck Wyatt."

"It's nice to meet you, sir," he said easily. "Katherine spoke highly of you." Glancing around, he noticed Hunter up on the ladder at the corner of the house. "Oh, hello. You're Hunter. You were at the Rusty Bucket the other day, weren't you? Katherine pointed you out to me."

"I was in town so I stopped by for lunch."

"I can see why—it's a great place to eat." Looking from him to Buck and back again, he frowned. "So what are you doing?"

"Just putting in a security light," he said easily.

He and Buck and John had already decided that they wouldn't mention the cameras they were installing with the security lights to anyone outside of the family. The cameras were small and virtually undetectable to anyone who didn't know what they were looking for. And Kurt Russell hardly spared the lights a look. Hunter sincerely doubted that the man would know a security camera if he tripped over it.

"Katherine's around here somewhere," he told him. "She was in the kitchen—"

"Buck, Rainey was wondering—" Stepping through

the front door, Katherine stopped short at the sight of Kurt. "Oh, my God! Lunch!"

Kurt grinned. "You forgot, didn't you?"

"I'm sorry. We had a—" she grimaced "—situation here last night, and we're still dealing with it."

"'Situation'?" he repeated with a frown. "What kind of situation?"

"We were robbed," Buck said flatly. "Someone took Katherine's watch right off her nightstand while she was sleeping."

"They also stole Elizabeth's diamond earrings," Hunter said. "And took a key to the house. Katherine's helping John and Elizabeth and Rainey change the locks while Buck and I install security lights."

"With everything that was going on, I completely forgot about our date," she added. "I'm sorry."

"Are you kidding? Don't give it a second thought." Stepping toward her, his face full of concern, he reached for her. "Are you all right? My God, you must have been scared out of your mind!"

"Actually, I'll probably be more scared tonight," she said as he hugged her.

Confused, he stepped back to frown down at her. "Why do you say that?"

"Because all this time, with everything that's been going on, I thought Hunter was playing a joke on me. Now that I know he wasn't the one moving things around in my room—"

"What? How long as this been going on?"

"Oh, for a week or more," Hunter replied. "She actually thought I was playing around with her underwear." He watched the other man's eyes narrow and couldn't resist the urge to needle him some more. "I told her I wouldn't come into her room until she asked me, but she didn't believe me. I can't imagine why. Just because I kissed her—"

"Hunter!"

"It was just a kiss," he told Kurt with a grin. "What's the big deal?"

Shooting him a withering look, Katherine wanted to shake him. Oh, he was enjoying himself, she thought, irritated. Did he think she didn't know that he was trying to drive Kurt away? It wasn't going to happen, dammit. She barely knew the man, didn't know if she wanted to continue seeing him, but that was her decision to make, not Hunter's. And when she got him alone, she would make sure he understood that. Then, if that didn't work, she was going to read the man the riot act. Who the hell did he think he was?

"I'm sure Kurt's not interested in one of your teasing pranks. They meant absolutely nothing," she retorted. "He was asking about the robbery, in case you hadn't noticed."

Taking his cue from her, Kurt said, "That's right. What about the jewelry? Does the sheriff think he can recover it?"

She shrugged. "The deputy who came out in the morning couldn't give us an answer. He's going to check the pawnshops and Internet, but he didn't hold out much hope."

"And he's sure the perp took the jewelry with him? How does he know? He could have hidden it somewhere on the property."

Buck frowned. "Why would he do that?"

"So he wouldn't get caught with it," he explained.

"He could come back later, in a couple of weeks, after everything has died down and there's no longer much hope of recovering it. By then the authorities would think he and the jewelry were long gone and probably wouldn't even be looking for him. And then there's the other possibility."

"Which is?" Katherine asked.

"Whoever took the jewelry might not have really been interested in stealing it at all. They might just be trying to scare you into leaving the ranch. I've been reading about it in the paper—you've had a hell of a lot of problems since you inherited the ranch. Violence hasn't worked, so maybe now, whoever wants to get their hands on this place has changed tactics. They're going to scare you by walking through the house at will, taking things, until you're afraid to close your eyes at night. A person like that wouldn't give a damn about a watch or a pair of diamond earrings. He's after bigger fish—the ranch."

As much as Hunter hated to admit it, the jackass had a point. "So what are you saying?" he growled. "We should search the ranch?"

"It wouldn't hurt," he said. "What have you got to lose?"

Hunter exchanged a look with Buck, who hesitated only a moment before nodding. "You may be right. It's worth a shot, anyway."

"I'll get the others," Katherine said, and hurried into the house.

Less than ten minutes later, the entire family spread out throughout the compound, searching the house and barn and foreman's cabin for Elizabeth's and Katherine's jewelry. Watching Kurt across the compound as he searched the flower gardens, Hunter tried to figure out what it was about the man he didn't like. It was more than just being too smooth with the ladies. In his years in intelligence, then as a P.I., Hunter had learned the hard way to trust his instincts. And every instinct he had told him that Kurt Russell was nothing but a lying sack of garbage. All he needed was a fingerprint, one fingerprint from the jerk—and he could find out every con Russell ever pulled. Unfortunately, he didn't have a fingerprint.

"Find anything?" John asked as he finished searching another garden at the corner of the house and moved to join him.

"No," he said with a grimace. "And neither did Romeo. You know, I can't figure out that bastard. What do you think he's up to?"

"I don't know. I've been trying to figure that out myself. Why is he so interested in what's going on here at the ranch? This is only the second time he's even laid eyes on Katherine. What's he doing? Playing Prince Charming?"

"I guess. And Kat seems to be eating it up with a spoon. I thought she was smarter than that. She certainly seems to have my number."

John chuckled. "That's because you pester the hell out of her. She doesn't have any choice but to stand up to you. Otherwise, you'd flatten her."

"True," he agreed with a chuckle. "I always did like a woman with sass."

"You'd better watch her," his brother warned. "She's a Wyatt, and I can tell you from experience that Wyatt women are hard to resist. When you least expect it, they'll steal your heart right out of your chest."

"Not me," he retorted. "I'm tougher than that."

"Yeah, yeah," John retorted. "That's what they all say. C'mon, help me search the barn."

He didn't have to ask Hunter twice. Happy to put some distance between himself and Katherine and her date, he followed John into the barn.

They'd hardly taken two steps inside, however, when they heard Kurt yell, "Oh, my God!"

Chapter 7

Kurt's cry echoed through the compound like a fire alarm. Everyone came running...just in time to see Katherine's date pull the missing jewelry—and her nightgown—from Hunter's 4Runner.

"What the hell?"

"This has to be a mistake!"

"If this is someone's idea of a joke—"

"Somebody must have planted them there."

His expression a study in innocence as the Wyatts all glared at him like he was some kind of pariah, Kurt said, "What? Why are you looking at me like that? Whose vehicle is this?"

"It's mine," Hunter growled, "though I'm sure you know that."

"Me? How would I know what you drive? I was just

looking for the stolen jewelry and decided to check all the vehicles."

Hunter snorted. "Yeah, right." Too late, he realized that Kurt was not only the one who took the jewelry and Katherine's nightgown, but the jackass had also set him up to take the fall. He never should have taken his eyes off him. He'd known there was something about Russell he didn't trust, and like a fool he'd dropped his guard.

"For the record," he told Kurt coldly, "I didn't take any of those things."

"Of course you didn't," his brother said angrily. "Anyone who would think that is an idiot."

"That's right," Katherine retorted, coming to Hunter's defense. "You drive me crazy, but you're not a thief, just a pest. Someone obviously planted those things there."

"Obviously," Hunter said dryly, looking at Kurt pointedly. "But we still have to call the sheriff. Kurt, I'm sure you'd like to do the honors."

"Hey, I'm not the bad guy here," he said defensively. "I'm just the messenger. You're the thief—"

"Stop right there," Buck told him icily. "Hunter was obviously set up—"

"Are you sure about that?" Kurt cut in. "According to Katherine, someone moved things around in her bedroom a couple of days ago. He readily admitted that he's kissed her. What else has he done? Is he staying in the house or a cabin somewhere on the ranch? Does he know where her room is? Tell me again why he didn't do this?"

"None of us have to tell you anything," Rainey said, stung. "I'm sorry, Katherine," she told her sister-in-law, "I don't mean to be critical of your date, but he's sticking his nose into something that's none of his business. He's not family. You hardly know him. What happens here is none of his business."

"You really are stepping over the line," Katherine told Kurt. "We appreciate your help in the search, but we all know Hunter didn't take anything. He's not that kind of man."

"I appreciate the vote of confidence," Hunter said gruffly, "but I'm still calling the sheriff." The matter settled, he pulled out his cell phone and punched in 911.

"This better be good," Sheriff Sherm Clark said as he stepped out of his cruiser to confront the Wyatts and their guests. "One of my deputies was just out here this morning. What the hell's going on now?"

"My sisters' jewelry was found," Buck told him.

"In my 4Runner," Hunter added grimly.

When the sheriff lifted a gray brow at that, Katherine snapped, "He had nothing to do with the robbery, Sheriff. He's not that kind of person."

"And how do you know that, missy?"

Her eyes narrowed at that. "I beg your pardon? My name is either Ms. Wyatt or Katherine—"

"Or Kitty-Kat," Hunter confided to the sheriff. "She hates that, though, so I wouldn't use that one if I were you."

"Dammit, Hunter, this is serious!"

"She's right," John told his brother. "Quit joking around. Someone's trying to frame you."

Frowning, the sheriff cut them all off with a muttered curse. "Will someone please tell me what the hell is going on? If you don't think Mr. Sinclair is responsible for the theft, why'd you call me?"

"Because I didn't do it," Hunter retorted, "but someone wants everyone to think that I did. The jewelry needs to be checked for fingerprints—"

"So what are you saying?" Kurt demanded. "That I stole it? My prints are on the damn things! I found them, for God's sake!"

"I don't believe anyone pointed the finger at you, Kurt," Katherine said quietly. "We're just trying to get at the truth."

Put on the spot in front of everyone, he had the good sense to quickly backpedal. "I've offended you, haven't I?"

"No, of course not—"

"Yes, I have—I can see it in your eyes. You think I'm out to get Hunter."

"No, I don't. Why would I? You found my watch and Elizabeth's earrings. We're grateful—"

"Even if Hunter's implicated?"

"I'm not implicated by anything," Hunter snapped. "I told you—"

"Enough," the sheriff growled. "Where's the jewelry and the nightgown? I'll just check everything for prints and see what we come up with."

"Deputy Marshall already checked Katherine's room and the cabin this morning," Elizabeth pointed out. "He didn't find anything."

"I'll check it again," he retorted. "Just to be safe. While I'm doing that, I'd appreciate it if you would all check your things to see if anything else is missing so I don't have to send a third car out here an hour from now. There are other problem areas in the county, you know. I can't tie up all my deputies at the Broken Arrow."

"We understand," Buck said, fighting back a smile. "As far as I know, nothing else is missing, but we'll do a thorough search just to make sure."

They all scattered…except Hunter and Kurt. Irritation flashing in his eyes, Kurt said, "Don't you need to check your things?"

"I don't have anything of value with me," he retorted. "Anyway, I'd rather stay here and watch you."

In the process of dusting the jewelry for prints, the sheriff looked up sharply. "You don't trust him?"

"Not as far as I can throw him."

"Why?"

Hunter shrugged. "Just a gut feeling. And my gut's never wrong."

"Neither is mine," Kurt said coldly. "And I know a womanizer when I see one. You're after Katherine, and you know it."

"So? You are, too, aren't you? Or am I mistaken? If you're not interested in her, what are you doing here? Why are you pursuing her?"

"My relationship with Katherine is none of your business."

"That's one way of not giving an answer," Hunter taunted. "Who are you? What are you up to?"

"I'd like to know that, myself," Sheriff Clark said, studying the other man with a frown.

"Here's my driver's license. Feel free to check me out." Kurt smirked.

He jerked his driver's license out of his wallet and held it out to the sheriff, who studied it with a frown. Stepping over to his cruiser, he called in Kurt's driver's license number, but when he rejoined both men a few minutes later, he said, "Looks like you're wrong, Mr. Sinclair. He doesn't have a record."

Kurt grinned triumphantly. "Any more objections?"

"Plenty," Hunter replied. "And time will tell if I'm right."

The matter apparently settled as far as the sheriff was concerned, he said flatly, "There's a latent print on the watch, but not enough to do anything with. As soon as I check the cabin and Katherine's bedroom, I'm out of here."

"You need to check Sinclair's room," Kurt objected. "He's the suspect, not Katherine or Elizabeth."

The sheriff gave him a narrow-eyed look that warned him he was pushing his luck. "I'll decide who's a suspect and who's not, young man. I'm the sheriff, not you, and I can do any damn thing I want. Understood?"

For a moment, Hunter thought the other man was going to be stupid enough to argue. He certainly thought about it before he finally nodded. Without another word, the sheriff strode into the house. Muttering a curse, Kurt followed, and Hunter was right on his heels. He didn't intend to let the jackass out of his sight.

Fifteen minutes later the sheriff appeared in the living room, where the family had gathered to wait while he finished his investigation. They all stiffened at the sight of his grim expression. "I found some prints."

"What?"

"Are you kidding?"

"Where?"

"All over the top of Elizabeth's jewelry box," he replied. "Naturally, the odds are that they're Elizabeth's, but just to be sure, I want everyone to come into the office to be fingerprinted." Casting a sharp look at Hunter and Kurt, he added, "I mean everyone."

Smirking, Kurt taunted, "Looks like you're fried, Sinclair. Hope you've got an alibi."

Exchanging a look with his brother and Buck, Hunter laughed. "Actually, I do," he said easily. "I played poker with Buck and John all night."

"You're lying."

"Watch it," Buck warned Kurt as Katherine and Elizabeth both gasped. "You're about to cross a line and have yourself thrown off this ranch, Mr. Russell. I don't know if you're a liar, but I know Hunter isn't. He did play poker with me and John all night. We shut down the game at eight o'clock this morning, then Buck cooked breakfast for the entire family. He hasn't been out of sight of a member of the family since we saw the lights in the cemetery last night."

"So the fingerprints on the top of Elizabeth's jewelry box obviously aren't his," Katherine chimed in, frowning at Kurt. "I don't know why you thought they would be. If he took the jewelry, do you really think he'd hide it in his car? He may be irritating as hell, but he's not stupid, Kurt. No one's that stupid. Why would you think he was?"

"Yeah," Hunter taunted, "why would you think I was stupid? I'm three steps ahead of you, Einstein. Or didn't you realize that?"

Kurt started to snap back, only to shut his mouth with an audible click of his teeth. "I didn't say he took anything," he finally said tightly. "I just think it's odd that everything started happening after he made a move on Katherine. I don't believe in coincidence."

"Then you'd better take a good hard look at yourself, buddy," Hunter told him coldly. "In case you haven't done the math, all this started after *you* came on the scene."

"All right, that's enough," Katherine said, stepping between them. "This is the first time Kurt's been to the house. He didn't even know my last name until a few days ago, so he couldn't possibly have known where I lived. I just gave him the address the other day. So now, that that's settled," she said when Hunter started to put in his two cents, "we need to go into town to be fingerprinted. Buck, I'll ride with you and Rainey, if you don't mind."

A small smile tugged at her brother's mouth. "That's fine with me. We're ready when you are."

"Then let's go," she said. And without another word, she walked out, leaving the others to follow as they would.

An hour later, after everyone was fingerprinted in the sheriff's office, they were free to go. Obviously realizing that he'd ticked her off, Kurt pulled Katherine aside and said huskily, "I'm really sorry if I offended you. I'm just worried about you. I really like you, and it bothers me that Hunter is taking advantage of you."

"No one's taking advantage of anyone," she said stiffly. Why did he and Hunter have to put her in the middle? She hated it, not that either one of them seemed to care. They were too busy sparring back and forth, trying to score points off each other. "In case you hadn't noticed, I'm a big girl," she informed him. "I can take care of myself."

He grimaced. "I know. Really," he insisted when she

gave him a skeptical look. "I don't blame you for being mad. Will it make you feel better if I tell you it will never happen again? Because it won't," he promised her. "This is your business, not mine, and if you believe that Hunter had nothing to do with your missing things, then that's good enough for me. Okay? Forgive me? Please?"

He was a man who knew how to charm a woman into forgetting her anger—she was very well aware of that—but there was also no doubting his sincerity. Her frustration melting, she couldn't help but smile as she said, "Okay, okay. You're forgiven. I appreciate the apology."

"You deserve it," he said simply. "So...how about lunch? Are we still on? I'd still love to take you to Aspen, but I understand if you'd rather not do that right now. After everything that's happened, I understand if you'd rather stick close to home."

"I really would," she admitted. "Thank you for understanding."

"No problem," he said easily. "Why don't we go get a hamburger? There's a great little place on the edge of town. Ham's Burgers. Get it? Ham's Burgers— Hamburgers?"

"I get it," she laughed. "Let me tell Buck, and we can go."

She expected Buck to warn her against going anywhere with Kurt, but all he said was, "Have you got your cell phone? You know where I am if you need me."

Touched, she gave him a quick hug. "Thanks. I'll see you later."

Her eyes locked with Hunter's as she turned to go, but he didn't say a word. She half expected him to follow her and Kurt to the restaurant, so he could watch Kurt like a hawk, but to her surprise, he didn't. When they reached the restaurant and took a seat in one of the booths near the front windows, Hunter was nowhere to be found.

She should have been relieved. Instead she was, to her surprise, disappointed. After the way he'd talked about Kurt, the obvious distrust he'd voiced, she'd felt sure he wouldn't leave her alone with the man. So where was he? What was going on?

"He's not here."

Gazing out the window, searching the cars in the parking lot, she hardly heard Kurt. Then his words registered. Glancing sharply at him, she frowned. "Who?"

"Sinclair. That is who you're looking for, isn't it?"

Heat stung her cheeks, but she faced him squarely. "He's so paranoid about you," she said with a shrug that wasn't nearly as casual as she'd hoped, "I just thought he'd be here."

"Don't be taken in by the man, Katherine," he warned.

Her elbows on the table, she propped her chin in the palms of her hands and frowned at him curiously. "Just what kind of man do you think he is?"

"He's part of your extended family," he said evasively. "I hate to say anything negative—"

"Don't let that stop you. Really," she assured him. "I want to know what you think. What's your problem with Hunter? You both seem to feel the same way about each other. I want to know why."

"He's a player," he said flatly. "He's cocky, arrogant, the kind of man who sees women as a notch on his belt. If you make the mistake of trusting him, he'll hurt you."

Katherine didn't see Hunter that way. Oh, he was a flirt, but she didn't see him as the kind of man who disrespected women the way Kurt described. That, however, was something she kept to herself. She didn't have to defend her opinion of Hunter. And she certainly didn't want to talk about him when she was on a date with another man.

"I'll be careful," she promised. "Enough about Hunter. I want to know more about you. What are you looking for in a woman?"

"That's easy," he replied, flashing her a smile she was sure he'd charmed countless women with. "You."

Parked two blocks down the street and partially hidden by a huge delivery van, Hunter checked his watch for the third time in five minutes and swore. How long did it take to eat a damn hamburger? Katherine and Kurt had been in the restaurant for well over an hour and there was no sign of them. Did they know he was watching? Had Russell convinced her to slip out the back door?

Five minutes, he told himself grimly. He was giving them five minutes, then he was going in.

Caught up in his thoughts, he almost didn't see Katherine step out of the restaurant with Russell right behind her. Then a car coming from the opposite direction honked when Katherine started to step off the curb to cross the street. She quickly stepped back, laughed at something Kurt said, then made sure no one was coming from either direction before crossing the street to where Kurt's car was parked.

Reaching for his cell phone, Hunter punched in

Buck's number. "They're getting in the car right now," he said by way of a greeting. "They should be heading your way any minute. I'll see you later tonight."

"Call me as soon as you know something," Buck said. "And be careful. I'm beginning to think this guy's capable of just about anything."

"Don't worry," he assured him. "I've had experience with jerks like Kurt more times than I can count. I'm watching my back. You just watch Katherine."

Hanging up, he made a sharp U-turn and headed the opposite direction. A glance in his rearview mirror assured him that Kurt and Katherine were already out of sight. Buck would keep her safe and see that she went directly home. In the meantime, he had work to do.

Reaching the main highway east of town, he turned south...toward Grady, where Kurt claimed to live on a ranch half the size of Texas. Yeah, right, Hunter thought jeeringly. If the jackass owned anything larger than a shoebox, then he was Donald Trump.

Another P.I. might have skipped a trip to Grady. A search on the Internet had turned up nothing on Russell—that didn't mean he didn't live there. Con men knew how to cover their bases, and if Russell didn't want anyone to check him out, he would have found a way to erase tidbits of info he didn't want on the Internet. Could he convince an entire town to verify his story? He'd have to see it to believe it, Hunter thought grimly. That was what today was all about.

An hour later, he arrived in Grady. As far as towns went, it wasn't much of one. A hundred people couldn't live there. There was a church, three bars and a ranch-supply store. A convenience store near the center of town sold groceries and gasoline, and the cemetery in the shadow of the church was nearly filled with tombstones that spanned generations. That was it.

Hunter went to the ranch-supply store. If Kurt's ranch was nearby, he would be known there, Hunter decided. But when he strode inside and casually asked directions to Kurt's ranch, no one had heard of him or the Russell Ranch. Further checking at all the local bars proved equally fruitless. Within an hour, it became obvious that no one who lived within a fifty-mile radius of Grady knew anything about a man named Kurt Russell or the Russell Ranch.

Everything Kurt had told Katherine about himself had been nothing but a lie, just as Hunter had suspected. Now that he had proof, it was time to tell Katherine and the family, not to mention the sheriff. His expression set in grim lines, he turned around and headed back to the Broken Arrow.

Katherine was the last to arrive in the living room for the family meeting that was scheduled for seven o'clock that evening. Rushing in, she frowned. "I didn't know we were having a family meeting. What's going on? Who called it?"

"I did," Hunter said as he strode into the room. "I need to talk to all of you."

Katherine rolled her eyes. "If this is about Kurt—"

"Actually, it is, but it's also about me. There's something you all need to know."

"You're not taking the job in California," his brother said with a grin. "I knew you wouldn't. It's not your scene at all."

"Actually," he said bluntly, "there never was a job in California." When everyone just looked at him, stunned, he admitted, "I just used that as a ruse to visit for a while."

"You didn't need an excuse to visit," Elizabeth told him, puzzled. "You're John's brother. You can stay as long as you like."

"I know. And thank you for saying that, but what I meant was that I couldn't stay an extended time without raising any suspicions. So I used the excuse of the California job."

"So why did you need an excuse?" Buck asked. "What's going on?"

"I'm a private investigator," he replied, and watched the surprise bloom on their faces. "When John told me he'd been shot and that something was going on here at the ranch, I decided to investigate what it was. I couldn't be nearly as effective if everyone knew what I did."

Katherine blinked in surprise. "You've been investigating us?"

"Not you. Well, not directly," he amended. "Kurt Russell—or whatever the hell his name is—now, that's another matter."

"What did you find out?" Buck asked.

"That he doesn't exist."

"I knew it!" John exclaimed. "The guy's too... smarmy." When Katherine shot him a look of surprise, he said, "Sorry, Kat, but the man's got con written all over him."

"But I thought you liked him."

"He was your date," Elizabeth said quietly. "Your

choice. We didn't want to interfere unless it was absolutely necessary."

"Apparently, Hunter didn't feel the same way," Katherine said bitterly. "Thanks a lot."

If she expected him to apologize, she was in for a rude awakening. "I was just doing my job. And yes, I know, no one hired me to check him out," he added, "but you do what you can for extended family."

"We're *not* family," she retorted. "And what do you mean, *'he doesn't exist'*?"

She was pale and more than a little bit shaken, but Hunter was relieved to see that her eyes were free of hurt. So she hadn't fallen in love with the jerk, he thought. At least she wouldn't hate him for exposing him for what he was.

"No one in Grady, Colorado, has ever heard of Kurt Russell or the Russell Ranch. It's a small town, Kitty-Kat. If he lived there, especially on a ranch the size of the one he described, someone would know him."

Confused, she frowned. "So if he doesn't live in Grady, and Kurt Russell isn't his real name, who is he?"

He shrugged. "I don't know. I haven't discovered that yet. We'll know more after the sheriff gets the report back on the fingerprint he found on your jewelry box."

"So you think he took the jewelry?" Rainey asked with a frown.

"I know he did," he replied. "He knew exactly where the jewelry was and led the sheriff right to it. And he did everything he could to throw the blame on me. I can't prove it, but, yeah, he did it," he said grimly. "Now we have to figure out why."

"Obviously, he sees you as a threat," Elizabeth said. "He knows you see through his story."

Pale and shaken, Katherine hugged herself. "*I* should have seen through his story. How could I have been so stupid?"

"You aren't the first woman to believe a con man," Hunter told her quietly. "It happens all the time."

"Well, it won't anymore," she retorted. "I'm done with the lying son of a dog. I wouldn't have gone out with him in the first place if you hadn't opened your big mouth."

Surprised, he blinked. "*Me?* So now it's *my* fault? What did I have to do with it?"

"You told the whole family that the only men I would meet on the Internet were losers. I hated to admit that you were right. I had to prove you wrong."

Later, Hunter knew he was going to enjoy that admission, but for now he had other concerns. "You can't let him know you distrust him when he asks you out again," he warned.

"Are you saying I should still date him?"

"No! Just be very careful in the way you break things off with him. We don't know anything about this guy except that he's got an agenda. He could hurt you."

Chapter 8

"**I**'ll call him right now."

"You don't have to do that," Elizabeth said, a worried frown knitting her brow. "Wait until he calls you again. Who knows? He may not."

"That's right," Rainey said. "We all made it pretty obvious that we didn't trust him. He had to realize he's not really welcome here."

"That might scare off some men," Buck agreed, "but I'm not sure about Russell. There's something in his eyes. I think he's dangerous."

"Then the sooner I end things, the better," she said, and reached for the phone.

Her stomach in knots, she told herself to not say anything derogatory against him, to lay the blame on herself so he would have no reason to resent her. But when he answered the phone, a cold chill squeezed her throat at the sound of his voice. Every instinct she had urged her to hang up.

"Hello? Katherine, is that you?"

Trapped, she said hoarsely, "Yes. I'm sorry—my throat just seemed to close up. How are you?"

"I'm fine. I wasn't expecting to hear from you tonight. Everything okay?"

She hesitated. Now what did she say? "I just wanted to talk to you. I've been thinking—"

"You don't want to go out anymore."

He said it flatly, with no emotion, and stopped her heart. "It isn't you," she said quickly. "You're a great guy and I really enjoyed getting to know you, but I just don't think I'm ready to date again. I can't stop thinking of Nigel. I'm still in love with him."

"The best way to get over a old love is to find a new one," he pointed out. "You can't do that if you hibernate at home and don't see anyone."

"I know," she agreed, "but first I have to give myself time to grieve. I hope you understand."

He hesitated, only to say, "Of course I understand. I've been where you are. You need some time. There's nothing wrong with that. I just hate to lose a chance to get to know you better. If you change your mind—"

"You'll be the first person I call," she promised, and quickly hung up. Wilting in relief, she turned to her family and Hunter. "Well? How'd I do?"

"Great!"

"Are you really still in love with Nigel?"

Biting out a filthy curse, Elliot Fletcher slammed his cordless phone back on the charger, only to grab it and throw it across the living room of his dingy apartment. "Damn bitch! She's ruining everything!"

What the hell was he going to do? he wondered furiously. He'd already received a sizable down payment to drive the Wyatts away, and the deadline that he'd been given was quickly slipping through his fingers. He could almost hear the clock ticking.

He hated not being in control. He should have had this done by now. But the damn Wyatts changed the locks and installed security lights. Bastards! How the hell was he going to get them away from the ranch for two nights in a row when none of the local wannabe heirs had managed to drive them away?

The phone rang then, and he almost didn't answer it. He wasn't in the mood to talk to anyone. But after ten rings, it was obvious that the caller had no intention of hanging up. Swearing, he strode over to the corner to retrieve the phone.

"What?" he growled.

The caller wasn't the least intimidated by his out of patience snarl. "You're pitiful. D'you know that? I've never seen someone so inept in my life."

Recognizing the mechanical voice of the sinister *employer* who'd hired him to run off the Wyatts, he felt his blood run cold. "It's not my fault—"

"The hell it isn't," the caller said icily. "I'm paying you a lot of money, and all I'm getting is mediocrity."

"I just need a little more time."

"Oh, you're going to get it," the voice assured him. "And this time, you're going to do it right, or you're history. Understood?"

"Y-yes, of course."

"And just to make sure there are no screwups this time, you're going to do exactly as you're told. Agreed?"

He had no choice. The cold, mechanical voice at the other end of the line was all the more sinister for the fact that it was so inhuman. Elliot liked to think there wasn't a hell of a lot he was scared of, but he wasn't a fool. If he wanted to live to see the weekend, he'd shut his mouth and follow orders.

"Agreed," he said with a confidence that even to his own ears sounded weak. "Just tell me what you want me to do."

Disgusted with herself for ever giving Kurt the time of day, Katherine hardly slept that night. The next day she was still kicking herself.

"I can't believe I was so stupid!" she grumbled to herself as she irritably pulled weeds in the rose garden. "I knew there was something about the jackass that didn't quite add up, something I couldn't put my finger on that made me slightly uncomfortable, but I never suspected every word out of his damn mouth was a lie. Talk about dumb!"

Quietly stepping into the rose garden in time to hear Katherine chew herself out, Hunter grinned. "Quit being so hard on yourself. You're not the first woman who's been taken in by a liar. Suck it up and be thankful you weren't in love with the jackass."

"That would be fine if this wasn't the second time a liar got the better of me," she retorted, jerking another weed out of the garden. "When am I going to wake up? First a married man with children, then a con man everyone saw through except me. What's wrong with me?"

"You're too damn trusting," he said promptly. "So what? You want me to sue you?"

"Dammit, Hunter, I'm serious!"

"No," he corrected her, "you're angry. Good. You should be. Next time, you won't be so quick to fall for a sad story."

"You got that right. I don't think I'll ever trust a man again."

"Sure you will," he chuckled. "When the time is right."

"The time's never going to be right. I'm going to die an old maid."

"Yeah, right," he said with a laugh. "And I'm going to grow up to be George Clooney. Now that we've got that settled, let's go for a ride."

In the process of reaching for another weed, she looked up in surprise. *"A ride?* Where?"

He shrugged. "I don't know. It doesn't matter. I just think you need to get away from the house for a while, go for a drive, get something to eat and just forget about everything."

She wanted to say yes so badly she could taste it. Which was, she told herself, exactly why she should say, Thanks, but no thanks. The man was just too darn attractive, and as much as she hated to admit it, she hadn't forgotten the kiss he'd given her in the Rusty Bucket. She still dreamed about it.

Shaken at the thought, she opened her mouth to say no and heard herself say instead, "I'd love to go. On one condition."

Interest—and amusement—sparked in his green eyes. "Really? And what condition would that be?"

"No flirting."

"Done."

She eyed him suspiciously. "Just that easily?"

"Yup," he said with a grin.

"With no strings attached?"

"I didn't say that."

"Hunter!"

"Kitty-Kat!"

She had to laugh at his tone, which exactly mimicked hers. "You're terrible. Are you ever serious?"

"Only when I have to be," he retorted. "So do you want to know what the strings are or not?".

What could she say? Of course she wanted to know! "Maybe."

"Maybe, huh? Is that the best you can do? C'mon," he teased, "where's your sense of adventure?"

A smart woman would have told him that she didn't have a sense of adventure, but he knew better. "Okay," she sighed, fighting a smile and losing, "name your strings."

"There's only one," he said with a grin. "I won't flirt if you wear something pretty and flirty. A dress."

"Really? You won't flirt like you are now?"

He grinned. "Nope. Scout's honor."

Her eyes narrowed suspiciously. "Right. And I'm supposed to believe that? Who just told me I was too damn trusting?"

"You're right," he said. "My mistake. It won't happen again...if you wear a dress."

"That's blackmail!"

Wicked mischief danced in his eyes. "Is it? So what are you going to do about it?"

"Make you regret you ever met me if you don't keep

your word," she promised with a grin as wicked as his. "Have I made myself clear?"

"Completely," he laughed. "Now, go change. We're wasting daylight."

Her heart pounding, she hurried up the stairs to her bedroom and pulled out a lemon-yellow sundress that Priscilla had designed for her last month. Frilly, as Hunter had requested, with a flowing skirt, spaghetti straps, and the lightest cotton she'd ever worn in her life, it was cool and beautiful and perfect to tease a man who'd promised not to flirt.

Grinning at the thought, she strapped on sandals, painted on her favorite lipstick and whisked her hair up off her neck with a clip. Observing herself in the mirror, she had to admit that she looked good. Refusing to ask herself why her heart was pounding with excitement, she headed downstairs.

Hunter took one look at her and started to whistle in appreciation. Almost immediately he stopped. "Sorry about that," he said with a grin. "You caught me by surprise. You look great!"

Holding out her skirt as if she was preparing to curtsy, she smiled. "I take it that this qualifies as flirty?"

"You got that right. C'mon, let's go!"

Katherine expected him to take her to the Rusty Bucket. It was, after all, the best restaurant in Willow Bend, and they had the best steaks in the county. If the decor was rough and left a lot to be desired, the food more than made up for it.

But when they reached Willow Bend, Hunter didn't even slow down as they approached the bar and grill. Instead, he drove right past it and headed out of town.

Surprised, she sat up straighter. "Hey! I thought we were going out to dinner."

"We are."

"Where? We just passed the Rusty Bucket!"

Amused, he said, "It's not the only place in the state of Colorado to eat. I thought we'd go somewhere else."

Frowning, she said, "Where?"

"Colorado Springs."

"Colorado Springs!"

"I told you you needed to get away for a while. This is your chance. So sit back, relax and enjoy yourself. I'll take care of everything."

She wanted to believe him, but he had that twinkle in his eyes, the one that always made her heart race and her stomach more than a little nervous. "That's what worries me," she said with a frown. "I'm not sure I trust you."

Far from worried, he only laughed. "I'm harmless."

"Yeah, right. I've heard that one before."

"Now, now," he teased, "don't be jaded. You're going to have a good time. Okay? Chill out."

She tried, but suddenly she felt as if she really was on a date, and she was about to receive a wonderful surprise. She was nervous and anxious and, dammit, excited. And it was all Hunter's fault. "Next time," she grumbled, "I'm going to ask more questions before I go anywhere with you."

"So there's going be a next time? Good, I'll start planning it."

"The next time I go for a *ride* with you," she corrected quickly. "That's all this is, Hunter—just a ride. So don't get carried away."

"Yes, ma'am," he said with twinkling eyes. "Whatever you say, ma'am."

Fighting a smile, she looked away, but that didn't make her any less aware of him. His attention was on his driving—he wasn't looking at her, wasn't even touching her. Still, she could feel the sexual energy emanating from the man. She didn't have to close her eyes to taste his kiss, to remember what it felt like to be in his arms. Her heart pounded, her blood heated, and deep inside she ached...

Suddenly realizing where her thoughts had wandered, she stiffened, but it was too late. In her mind, she'd stepped over an invisible line that divided a platonic outing with her sister's soon-to-be brother-in-law and a date. And there was no going back.

How had this happened? she wondered wildly. How had she let it happen? What had he done to her with nothing more than some teasing and a kiss?

Her thoughts chasing themselves in circles, searching for answers that weren't there, she hardly noticed the passage of time or miles. Then suddenly they were driving into Colorado Springs.

"I thought we'd get a snack now, then have dinner later, if that's all right with you," he told her, breaking the silence. "Unless, of course, you're starving."

"A snack's fine," she assured him. "What'd you have in mind? Ice cream or something?"

"Yeah...or maybe some popcorn...or both."

"Popcorn?" she echoed. "Where are we going to get popcorn?"

"Here," he said with a grin, and pulled into the parking lot of a movie theater. "There's a movie I've been wanting to see, and I was hoping you might want to see it with me."

"If we've got time, I'm game. What's the movie?"

"*Summer Wind.*"

Stunned, she blinked. "You want to see *Summer Wind?*"

"Yeah." His expression totally innocent, he arched a dark brow at her. "Why? Don't you?"

Studying him, she had to laugh. "You know, you're really good. If I didn't know better, I just might believe you."

"I don't know what you're talking about," he said with pretended loftiness. "Women aren't the only ones who like period art films."

How, she wondered, touched, had he known how badly she wanted to see *Summer Wind?* She hadn't said a word about it to anyone. "You don't have to do this," she said quietly. "I know it's probably the last thing you want to see."

"Then you don't know me very well," he said, taking her hand and linking his fingers with hers. "I'd sit and watch the caution light blink in Willow Bend if I had your hand in mine."

For a second she thought he was serious. His eyes met hers, and for once his wicked grin was nowhere in sight. Something caught at her heart, something she was afraid to examine too closely. Then the corner of his mouth twitched.

Not sure if she was relieved or disappointed, she rolled her eyes. "I knew it. You're flirting!"

His gaze skimmed the curve of her mouth. "No, I'm not."

"What do you mean...*no?* You know darn well you are."

"No, this is flirting," he said huskily, and leaned over to kiss her.

She should have pulled back—he gave her time. But she couldn't seem to move, couldn't resist the heat of his eyes, his mouth. His lips brushed hers, whisper soft, setting her blood humming. Then he was pulling back, and all she could think was that it hadn't lasted nearly long enough.

"So what do you think?"

Her senses reeling, she scowled at him. "What do I think? I think you're a dirty, rotten, low-down—"

"I get the drift," he said, laughing, and pushed open his car door. Coming around to open the passenger door for her, he grinned as she ignored the hand he held out to her and stepped down from the 4Runner. "Hey, where are you going?"

"To the movies," she retorted. "And you're not only paying, you're buying me whatever I want."

"Yes, ma'am," he chuckled, and caught up with her with three long strides.

The movie was an eighteenth-century period piece about two star-crossed lovers who were destined to have only one summer together before they were torn apart by war. Katherine had fallen in love with the story—and the characters—when she'd read the book, but even though she'd been eagerly anticipating the movie, she'd been afraid it could never live up to the magic of the book. She couldn't have been more wrong. From the beauty of the cinematography, costumes and sets to the chemistry between the hero and heroine as they found and lost love in the Carolinas during the American Revolution, everything about the movie was perfect. It tugged at the artist in her soul, and she loved it. But as she watched fate tear the couple on the screen apart, she was more aware than ever that the movie was most definitely a chick flick. And despite Hunter's claims to the contrary, she knew it was not the kind of movie he would have normally chosen to go see. He'd picked it strictly for her.

Touched, she glanced at him in the darkness of the theater, studying his profile as bombs exploded on the screen. Did he know what he did to her with such a simple act of kindness? Did he realize that her senses hummed every time he shifted in his seat next to her? That she couldn't forget how he'd kissed her in the car?

Frustrated, irritated with herself, she stared at the screen as the hero declared his undying love for the heroine. But every one of her nerve endings was attuned to Hunter. It seemed as though, from the moment she'd met him, he'd been a thorn in her side, needling her, driving her crazy. And now...he was still driving her crazy. What was going on? What was happening to her? What had he done to her?

Lost in her musings, she never noticed when he turned his gaze from the screen to her. She didn't see the banked heat in his eyes as he looked at her, didn't notice that he was content to just watch her. Then suddenly, with no warning, he leaned over and whispered in her ear, "Do you know how the story ends?"

His breath tickled her ear...and stole the air right out of her lungs. Heat licking her senses, she didn't even hear what he said. Dazed, she looked at him blankly. "What?"

For a split second she thought she caught the glint of mischief in his eyes, but then he leaned closer and she couldn't be sure. "How do you think it ends?" he said softly in her ear. "Do they get married and live happily ever after or does he get killed in the war?"

The thunder of her heart pounding loudly in her ears, she should have just shrugged and turned her attention back to the movie. Instead she leaned close and whispered, "I read the book, but the movie might have a different ending. You'll have to wait and find out."

Too late she realized she'd made a mistake. The scent of his cologne reached out to wrap around her, teasing her senses, making it nearly impossible to concentrate. When she shifted closer to ask another question and his shoulder brushed intimately with hers, her senses swam and she found it impossible to keep track of the movie's story line. All she could think of was Hunter...and the way he'd kissed her. She ached for him to do it again.

Distracted, she couldn't have said if the movie had the same ending as the book. Suddenly, the credits were rolling and she and Hunter were walking out of the theater, hand in hand.

When he led her to the 4Runner and opened the passenger door for her, she expected him to shut the door for her as soon as she was seated, but instead he leaned in to buckle her seat belt for her. In the time it took to draw in a surprised breath, his mouth was just inches from her.

Suddenly breathless, her eyes locked with his in the growing twilight. "Hunter—"

"I'm just making sure you're safe," he said quietly. "I wouldn't want anything to happen to you."

She was more than capable of buckling her own seat belt, and they both knew it. "You're flirting again."

"No, I'm not," he rasped, and covered her mouth with his.

She stiffened, expecting the same fleeting kiss he'd given her before. But there was no brush of the lips this time. This kiss was hot and seductive and deadly serious. His hungry mouth wooed and caressed and made it impossible for her to think. And when she gasped softly, his tongue swooped in, stealing the last of her sanity. She tried to remember why kissing him wasn't smart, but it was too late. She was already lost. With a moan that seemed to come from the center of her being, she wrapped her arms around him and kissed him back.

Lost to everything but each other, they never saw the two cars full of teenagers racing past them on the street...until they suddenly blared their horns. Startled, she and Hunter broke apart, and just that easily the moment was destroyed.

Later she couldn't have said how long they stared at each other. She wanted him to kiss her again—she'd never wanted anything so badly in her life. And that stunned her. This was Hunter. When had this happened?

"Guess we'd better get going," he said thickly. "It's getting late."

Dazed, disappointed, she was horrified to discover she was on the verge of tears as they headed for home. Then he reached for her hand and his fingers closed around hers. Just that easily he rekindled the heat of the kiss she could still taste on her lips, and in the near darkness, his eyes met hers. He didn't say a word, but he didn't have to. The message was loud and clear. The evening was far from over.

The next few hours passed in a blur. They stopped for something to eat, but she hardly noticed what she ate. Under the table, his foot played with hers, teasing her, making it impossible for her to think of anything but him. And when they returned to the 4Runner, her hand was once again in his. And for reasons she couldn't begin to understand, she was more content than she'd ever been in her life.

She could have ridden with her hand in his for the rest of the night. Later, she knew that would worry her—what was happening to her?—but for now, nothing else mattered, and she refused to ask herself why.

It was late when they arrived at the house, and she and Hunter both expected to find everyone in bed. Instead, every light in the house was on. Surprised, she frowned. "What's going on? Why's everyone still up?"

"Good question," Hunter said as he braked to a stop in the circular drive and cut the motor. "C'mon, let's go find out."

They hurried up the front steps, but before they reached the front door, Buck jerked it open. "Where the hell have you been?"

Shocked, Katherine said, "Excuse me?"

Looking more than a little frantic, he grimaced and immediately apologized for his sharp tone. "I'm sorry. I shouldn't have spoken to you that way. I've just been calling and calling and haven't been able to get you."

"We went to see a movie in Colorado Springs," Hunter told him. "Why? What's wrong? What's going on?"

"Priscilla's been in a car accident."

Chapter 9

Katherine blanched. "What? When? Is she all right? What happened?"

"I don't know the details of the accident," he said gruffly, "but she's in critical condition—"

"Oh, God! Buck—"

"I know," he said, pulling her into his arms for a hug. "I'm scared for her, too, but we have to believe she's going to be all right."

"What did the doctor say? Were you able to talk to her? Where's she hurt?"

Helpless, all he could do was shake his head. "I don't know. Someone from the hospital called—all they could say was that she was being rushed into surgery, and we should come if we can."

Horrified, Katherine choked back a sob. "Have you

called the airlines? Where's Elizabeth? Does she know? We have to pack."

"She's in the bathroom," John said quietly as he stepped into the front entry, joining them. "She's having a tough time dealing with this."

"Is she packed?" Katherine asked. "I've got to throw some things together. What time does our plane leave? We've got to get to the airport."

She started to step around Buck and run upstairs, but he immediately moved in front of her, blocking her path. "You and Elizabeth aren't going, sis. I'm just taking Rainey."

Surprised, she blurted out, "That's ridiculous! Of course we're going! Priscilla's hurt. She could be—"

Dying. She didn't say the word—her throat closed up just at the thought of it. "She's our sister, too, Buck," she choked. "Of course we're going."

"I know you want to go, and I hate telling you you can't, but we can't all be gone at once."

"Why the hell not?" she demanded. Then she remembered. "Oh, God, Hilda's will!"

Her eyes bloodshot from crying, Elizabeth joined them just in time to hear Katherine's groan of defeat. "I hate this!" she cried. "I hate being told by a stupid piece of paper that we can't go anywhere together. This is our ranch. We're Wyatts, dammit, and our great-great-great-grandfather started the damn thing. We're the last of the Wyatts. That should be enough for us to inherit."

A fleeting smile curled the corners of Buck's mouth. "You may have put one too many greats in there, but I get your point. And if Hilda hadn't written restrictions into her will, there would be no question that the ranch was ours and we could go and come as we please. Unfortunately, the property came with year-long strings, and if we want to inherit the Broken Arrow, we can't ignore them."

"There's no way the three of you can fly to London, check on Priscilla, then return to the ranch without being gone for at least two nights," Hunter pointed out. "It's physically impossible."

"We'd lose the ranch," Elizabeth reminded Katherine. "And if Priscilla's injuries are really serious, she could need our help for a long time. We'll have to work out a schedule among the three of us so one of us can always be with her until she's back on her feet."

"Or you'll bring her back here while she recovers and all of you will be here to help her," John said.

Katherine knew they were right, but how could she stay home when Priscilla was hurt? "She needs us *now*," she argued. "Now, when she's hurt and alone. Granted, we can't be there by the time she wakes up from surgery, but she still needs us—all of us. There must be a way..."

"No one really feels like having company after surgery," Hunter told her. "And remember...you don't know the nature of her injuries. I don't want to scare you, but if she's seriously hurt, there's a good possibility that she'll be unconscious for quite some time. If that's the case, she's not going to know who's there and who's not. By the time she does, the three of you will have worked out how you're going to take turns taking care of her."

She couldn't argue with his logic—but that did nothing to calm her fears. Images of her sister kept playing in her head…Priscilla slamming into another car…blood— there would have been a lot of blood and broken glass. Was she cut? Scarred for life? What if she was paralyzed? It could happen. It may have already happened.

Her heart stopped at the thought. *No!* she cried silently. This couldn't be happening. Not to Priscilla. She was her baby sister, two years younger, and they'd always been close. Just the thought of her being injured, possibly dying, scared her to death. She had no family there, yet, no one to help her, to speak for her if she couldn't speak for herself.

Tears welling in her eyes, she told Buck, "You'll call us as soon as you get there and you know she's all right? Promise? And you won't sugarcoat it? If she's really in bad shape, we need to know."

"I agree," he said huskily. "I promise I'll call you as soon as I see her, and I'll tell you everything. Okay?"

She didn't like it, but their hands were tied by the will. For now there was nothing else they could do. "I don't care how late it is…"

He smiled slightly. "Even if it's the middle of the night. Anything else?"

"Tell her we love her and we'll see her soon," Elizabeth said huskily. "And if she needs us there tomorrow, one of us can be there."

"I'll tell her," he promised. Giving them both a hug, he said, "I've got to go upstairs and help Rainey finish packing. Try not to worry. Okay? Everything's going to be all right."

Long after Buck and Rainey left, Katherine was too agitated to sit still, let alone go upstairs to bed. Pacing restlessly, she had never been so worried in her life. She couldn't stop her frantic thoughts...or stand the silence that echoed through the house with Buck's and Rainey's leave-taking.

"I hate this!" she exploded, shattering the silence. Prowling around the family room, picking up a picture of her and Priscilla, she blinked back the tears that spilled into her eyes and set the picture back down with a snap. "What are we supposed to do now? Watch a movie on television? Go to bed? While Priscilla may be dying? I don't think so!"

Hunter exchanged a look with John. "Why don't you and I whip up something to eat in the kitchen?" he told Katherine. "All we had for dinner was fast food, and that was hours ago. I don't know about you, but I could use some pancakes and sausage. How are you at making pancakes?"

"I'm not hungry."

"I realize that," he said, "but someone else may be. If you can handle the flapjacks, I'll do the sausage."

"I don't think I could make anything without burning it," she said honestly. "You'd just have to throw it out."

"This isn't about food," John told her quietly. "It's about finding a way to pass the time. Otherwise, you and Elizabeth are going to drive yourselves crazy with worry."

Tears filled her eyes at his words. "I know. I'm sorry. I just can't stop worrying."

"Nobody expects you and Elizabeth to do anything else," Hunter said, taking her hand. "C'mon, sweetheart, let's go see what damage we can do in the kitchen."

"Elizabeth and I will come, too," said John. "While

you two are working on the pancakes, we'll whip up a chocolate cake. Isn't that right, Lizzie? C'mon, honey, it'll take your mind off everything."

"All right," she choked. "But you have to let me cry if I feel like crying."

"You do whatever you have to do, honey," he said huskily, slipping an arm around her waist. "Just don't cry in the cake batter."

Leaning against him with a watery chuckle, she said, "I'll do my best."

An hour and a half later, a stack of leftover pancakes dripping in butter and syrup sat on the stove, along with a cake that only the men had tasted. Elizabeth and Katherine had found some comfort in a pot of tea, but as midnight came and went and minutes stretched into hours, they both had less and less to say. Pale and drawn, they spent long minutes at a time staring into space.

"How about poker?" John suggested suddenly. "The last time Lizzie and I played, she whipped my butt. I think it's time for a rematch."

"Sounds good to me," Hunter said, "but do I need to remind you that when you and I and Buck played the other night, I whipped your ass, too?"

"Yeah, right," his brother sniffed. "You never beat me at poker in your life."

"The hell I didn't! Where are the cards? I'll show you—"

For what seemed like the first time in hours, Katherine and Elizabeth both smiled. "Our father taught all of us to play poker when we were just kids," Elizabeth said, remembering. "We would have all-night poker parties, and it seemed like Priscilla won every time. She wouldn't seem to be paying attention at all—"

"And the next thing you knew, she was laying down a royal flush and she didn't even know what she had," Katherine chuckled. "She was so funny."

For a moment both sisters smiled at the memory... then at almost the same time, they remembered Priscilla's accident. Suddenly their eyes were swimming in tears.

"I'm sorry," Elizabeth choked, wiping at her streaming eyes, "but I can't do this anymore. I can't pretend—"

"Honey, you don't have to pretend anything," John said, starting toward her. "It's okay to cry."

"I know," she sniffed. "I'm just not very good company right now." Her tears suddenly spilling over her lashes, she said thickly, "I think I'll go back to the cabin and lie down until Buck calls."

"I'll go with you—"

"No, you don't have to. Really. I'm fine. I just need some time to myself right now."

He frowned, not liking that idea at all. "All right. But I won't be long—only about fifteen minutes."

Struggling with her own tears, Katherine said, "I think I'll go to bed, too, before I fall apart and make a fool of myself."

"It's okay to cry," Hunter told her, but that was as far as he got. Before he could stop her, she hurried out of the family room and rushed up the stairs.

For the first time since they'd learned of Priscilla's accident, John and Hunter found themselves alone. "You know we're not going to keep them away from London for very long," John said, breaking the silence.

"Especially if Priscilla's injuries are as serious as they appear to be. The second they know how she is, they're going to insist on seeing her for themselves."

"When the locals hear about this and realize the family's going to be juggling trips back and forth to London, there's going to be hell to pay," Hunter said flatly. "We're going to have to be ready for a full-out attack on the ranch."

His expression grim, John agreed. "I didn't want to say anything to the girls, but it's going to get ugly—"

From upstairs, a sudden bloodcurdling scream ripped through whatever he was going to say next, echoing through the house like something out of a horror movie. For a split second neither of them moved. Then, almost on the heels of Katherine's scream, they caught the faint traces of another scream, and this one came from the direction of the foreman's cabin. In the split second it took for them to realize that both women were in trouble, they were already running into Buck's office to grab rifles from the gun cabinet.

"This looks like the first attack," John growled. "Be careful!"

"As soon as I find out what's going on with Katherine and she's safe, I'll call on your cell," he yelled as his brother took off running for the cabin. "Watch your back!"

There was no time for a plan of attack, no time to even figure out what was going on. Katherine screamed again, and Hunter's heart stopped dead in his chest. Swearing, he took the stairs two at a time.

Feeling like he was running in quicksand, it seemed to take an eternity to reach the top of the stairs. Katherine didn't scream again, but that did little to reassure him. She couldn't scream if someone had knocked her out…killed her.

Something squeezed his heart at the thought, infuriating him. No, dammit! She wasn't dead, and anyone who even thought about hurting her was going to have to deal with him. When he got through with them, they'd be lucky if they had any teeth—or limbs—left.

He clenched his jaw on the fury that pulled at him, hesitating in the upstairs hallway as years of training kicked in. Glancing both ways to make sure no one was in the hall waiting to ambush him as he rushed to Katherine's rescue, he slipped out of his shoes and ran soundlessly down the hall in his socks.

The door was closed, but even as he reached for the door handle, he froze, listening. For a second he thought he heard Katherine whimper, but he couldn't be sure. Then she screamed again, turning his blood to ice. With a growl of rage, he kicked open the door and burst into her bedroom.

He expected to find her in the clutches of a monster intent on raping and killing her. But he saw at a glance that there was no one in the room but Katherine. Standing on the far side of the bedroom in the glow from the light on her nightstand, she was as white as the pristine sheets on her bed.

Stopping in his tracks, Hunter frowned in confusion. A blind man couldn't have missed the fear in her eyes, but he didn't see a damn thing to be afraid of. "What the hell's going on? Why'd you scream?"

"There's a snake in my bed!" she cried. "It almost bit me when I turned back the sheets."

"What kind of snake? Did you get a look at it?"

"I was so shocked…I'm not sure, but I think it's a rattlesnake."

Hunter swore. There was no sign of the snake, but he didn't intend to take any chances. "Move away from the bed," he growled. "It's probably in the covers."

Her gaze locked on where the sheet and bedspread had slipped halfway onto the floor, Katherine cautiously put more distance between herself and the bed. When she was well away from the snake's possible hiding place, Hunter flipped on the overhead light and stepped toward the bed.

Alarmed, she stiffened. "What are you doing? Stop!"

"Sweetheart, I've got to find the snake, and the only way I can do that is to pull the covers back."

"But it could bite you!"

"Don't worry," he said grimly. "I'm not planning on using my hand." Using the tip of the rifle, he carefully lifted the sheets and bedspread from the mattress.

The unmistakable sound of the snake's rattle was almost immediate.

"Oh, God," she whispered, and crowded closer to the corner, as far from the bed as possible.

"Easy," Hunter murmured, never taking his eyes from the bed as he slowly, carefully, continued to lift the bedding from the bed. "I'm not going to let it hurt you."

"I'm not worried about me," she retorted, watching in growing horror. "You're the one teasing a snake."

"I'm not teasing it," he replied in the same soft

murmur. "I'm killing it." And with no more warning than that, he whisked the covers from the bed, revealing the snake, which was coiled at the end of the mattress. Lightning quick, he tossed the end of the sheet off the rifle and fired.

Stunned, Katherine couldn't say how long she stood there, frozen, her gaze locked in horror on the dead snake. Then suddenly she was moving, at first stiffly, then running. Before the first tears spilled down her cheeks, she threw herself into Hunter's arms.

"I was so scared!"

"I know," he said, snatching her close. "But you're safe now."

"How did it get in here?"

"I don't know, but we'll have to check into it later," he said, already pulling her into the hallway. "We've got to check on Elizabeth."

"Elizabeth? Why?"

"Because she screamed at the same time you did."

Her heart in her throat, Katherine was right behind Hunter as they bolted down the stairs and ran for the back door. And with every step, she found herself praying aloud.

"Let her be all right. Please, please, let her be all right."

But when they burst out the back door, she knew she wasn't. As they ran around the corner of the barn, John stepped out of his cabin with Elizabeth in his arms. Her right wrist and hand were immobilized in a splint and there wasn't an ounce of color in either of their faces.

Horrified, Katherine ran to help, but she took one look at her sister and was afraid to touch her. Elizabeth couldn't keep her eyes open, sweat seemed to be pouring off of her, and her breathing was ragged.

"What happened?" Katherine cried, alarmed. "What's wrong with her?"

"S-snake," her sister gasped faintly.

Horrified, Katherine's knees threatened to buckle. "Oh, God!"

"Did you call an ambulance?" Hunter demanded, studying Elizabeth with a frown. "She must be allergic, John. She's having a damn severe reaction to the venom."

"I know," John said grimly. "That's why I tried to call an ambulance. The phone lines have been cut."

"What?"

Hunter bit out a curse. "We've got to get her to the hospital."

Cradling Elizabeth close, he held out the keys that were clutched tightly in his hand. "My truck's in the lean-to. Hurry."

He didn't have to tell Hunter twice. Death due to snakebites in the United States wasn't nearly as common as most people thought, but it happened. And he knew from personal experience, when he'd tangled with a rattler in Utah once, that even a young snake could make you feel like you were going to die. When you mixed in possible allergic reactions with that, anything could happen.

Sprinting to where the truck was parked in the lean-to that was attached to the barn, he started it with a sharp flick of his wrist, then threw it into Reverse. Backing out of the parking spot in a cloud of dust, he pulled up next to his brother and Elizabeth and jumped out to help them into the vehicle before it had barely shuddered to a stop.

"Easy," he murmured as he and John together lifted Elizabeth in the backseat. "The snake was in her bed, wasn't it?"

Shocked, John said, "How did you know?"

"Because there was one in Katherine's bed, too."

Caught up in her own pain until then, Elizabeth cried, "*What?* Did it bite her? Oh, God!"

"I'm all right," Katherine assured her quickly. Tears stinging her eyes, she squeezed Elizabeth's uninjured hand. "Hang on, Lizzie," she said huskily. "You're going to be all right, too, just as soon as we get you to a hospital."

As they pulled out of the driveway, Hunter said, "Katherine, call the hospital and let the emergency room know we're on our way so they can have the antivenin ready."

Already reaching for her phone, Katherine called information and within seconds, she was talking to one of the emergency room doctors. When she hung up, her face was pale. "The doctor said to watch for shock and possible blood if she throws up. John, he also wants you to check the swelling on her arm every fifteen minutes and mark it with a pen so he'll be able to see how fast the poison is progressing. And she needs to be as still as possible. Movement only draws the poison deeper into her body."

"There's a pen in the consol," John told her. "Hunter, turn the dome light on so I can see."

Never taking his eyes from the road, Hunter did as he requested. Glancing in the rearview mirror at his brother, he asked quietly, "How's the swelling?"

His eyes dark with worry, he met Hunter's gaze in the mirror. "Nearly up to her elbow."

His tone was even, without alarm, but Hunter and Katherine both heard the tension in his voice. Without a word, Hunter increased his speed.

The ride to Willow Bend was normally a twenty-minute drive, and that was during the day, when ranchers were out and about, slowing traffic. At one o'clock in the morning, there shouldn't have been a soul on the road. But when Hunter flattened the accelerator, pushing the speedometer to eighty, he had to hit the brakes almost immediately as he topped a hill and found himself bearing down on a beat-up old Ford sedan that only had one taillight and was almost invisible in the darkness.

Seated in the passenger seat, Katherine found herself reaching for a break pedal that wasn't there. "Watch it!"

"I know," he growled, never taking his eyes from the vehicle in front of him. "I see the jerk." Caught in the sharp glare of his headlights, the other driver had stark white hair and could hardly see over the steering wheel. "What the devil's the old geezer doing out at this time of night?"

"I think it's a little old lady," Katherine said with a frown. "She must have terrible night vision. She couldn't be going more than twenty kilometers an hour."

"We don't have time for this," Hunter retorted. "Hang on. I'm going to pass her."

But as he checked his mirrors to make sure the passing lane was clear, then started to swing over into the oncoming lane to pass the ancient Ford, the driver suddenly swung wide, too. In the blink of an eye, the Ford was straddling the middle line and cutting him off before he could even think about passing.

"Son of a—"

"What's she doing?"

"We've got to pick it up, Hunter," John said sharply from the backseat. "Lizzie's breathing's really becoming labored."

Hunter didn't wait to hear more. They were approaching a curve and the driver in front of him pulled back into the correct lane. Seeing no headlights coming around the curve, Hunter took a chance and punched the accelerator at the same time he jerked the wheel into the oncoming lane.

Surprised, the driver in front of them tried to pull over at the last second, but it was too late. Hunter shot around the Ford and back into his lane just as an eighteen-wheeler whizzed past them with its horn blaring. It missed them by mere inches.

"Oh, God!"

"Sorry about that," Hunter said quickly. "If I hadn't gotten by that old fart, we'd still be dragging behind her—if it even is a *her*—an hour from now. So batten down the hatches. We're going to fly." And with no other warning, he raced down the open road toward the lights of Willow Bend in the distance.

Chapter 10

The second Hunter braked at the emergency room entrance, a team of medical staff came running. Elizabeth was carefully transferred to a stretcher. A nurse questioned Katherine about her sister's medical history, while John gave the doctor the details of her reaction to the snakebite. Within seconds, Elizabeth, with John at her side, was whisked into one of the curtained cubicles of the emergency room, and Katherine and Hunter were left to cool their heels in the waiting room.

Unable to sit still, Katherine paced restlessly. "Do you think she'll be okay?" she asked worriedly. "She looked so pale. And did you see her hand? It was so swollen. Can a snakebite cause permanent damage?"

"The actual puncture area will bother her for a long time," he said honestly. "The venom does cause some tissue damage, but we got her to the hospital in a relatively short time period, so the damage should be minimal. She's going to be sick as a dog for a while, though."

That proved to be an understatement. Already weak as a kitten, Elizabeth vomited for two hours. The doctor ordered fluids to keep her hydrated, but other than that and the antivenin they'd already given her, there was little that could be done to help her through the ordeal. She just had to suffer through it.

It was nearly four in the morning when the doctor called Katherine and Hunter into the emergency room cubicle where John sat next to Elizabeth's bed, holding her hand. "Hopefully, you're past the worst of the vomiting," he told Elizabeth. "We're going to move you to a room—"

"I can't go home?"

"Absolutely not," he retorted firmly. "In fact, you're going to be with us awhile. At least three days."

"Three days!"

"I'm staying with her," John said flatly.

The doctor nodded. "That won't be a problem— there's a chair in the room that converts into a bed. Though, I'll warn you now that you're not going to get very much sleep. The nurses will be checking on her every fifteen minutes for the next few hours."

"That's all right," John replied. "I don't plan to sleep much anyway."

"Then I guess I'll see you later," the doctor said. "If you need anything, just tell the nurse."

Fifteen minutes later Elizabeth was transferred from the E.R. to a private room, and within minutes of settling into her hospital bed, she was sound asleep.

After everything she had been through, no one could blame her for passing out the first chance she got.

Seated at her side, John glanced from his brother to Katherine and said quietly, "Are you two going to stay here or go back to the house?"

Hugging herself, Katherine shuddered. "I'm not going back to the ranch until daylight, when I can check things out and make sure that whoever snuck into my room and your cabin hasn't planted any more snakes in the house."

Hunter exchanged a look with his brother. "She's right—there's no question they were planted. What I want to know is how the intruder got into the house and cabin without the dogs barking."

"We'll find out when we check the security cameras," John replied. "And you're right, I didn't even think about the dogs. You think they were drugged?"

"It's possible," he agreed. "Whoever put those snakes in the girls' beds has definitely stepped up their game. We're going to need to be on constant alert."

His face set in harsh lines, John said, "He's not the only one. As soon as I know who did this, I'm going to step up my game."

"I'll be right there with you," Hunter promised. Glancing over at Elizabeth, whose sleep was far from restful, he added quietly, "If the two of you are going to be here for at least three days, you're going to need some things from home. We'll pack a case for you."

"Just be careful."

"Don't worry," Hunter assured him. "I plan to carry a gun everywhere I go on the ranch from now on. And I'm damn sure going to discover how the bastard who planted those snakes got in the house. It's not going to happen again."

"Can we get you anything before we leave?" Katherine asked John. "The cafeteria's probably closed, but there's bound to be some vending machines somewhere around here."

"Actually, coffee sounds great," he told her, pulling some change from his pocket. "Thanks."

"I'll be right back," she promised.

The second the door swung shut behind her, John said quietly, "After everything that's happened, I didn't want to talk about this in front of Katherine, but I've been thinking about Priscilla's accident—"

"You think it's connected to the snakes?"

"I think Priscilla's accident wasn't an accident at all."

"If that's the case, then someone has some damn long connections," Hunter retorted. "We need to call Buck and warn him."

"I agree." Reaching for his phone, he punched in the number to Buck's cell phone. Almost immediately, however, it went to voice mail. Leaving a quick message for Buck to call him on his cell phone as soon as possible, he hung up and told Hunter, "His phone's still off. They haven't landed yet."

Glancing to where Elizabeth lay in bed, Hunter frowned. "Are you going to tell Lizzie about this?"

"Not right now. She's got enough to worry about without adding this on top of it. I'll tell her when she's stronger and back on her feet. What about Katherine? She won't appreciate being kept in the dark."

She would, Hunter thought, be madder than a wet

hen. "I'll tell her later today, when we know what's going on with Priscilla and Elizabeth is doing better. Not that she can do anything about it," he added in disgust. "Whoever's organizing this crap is one step ahead of us. We've got to come up with a plan to beat them at their own game."

"Good luck," John retorted. "I've been trying for months now to anticipate where the next attack is coming from, and it's impossible. I don't even know how many jackasses we're dealing with. It seems like the whole damn town's involved."

"And they could all be acting independently." Hunter groaned at the thought. "Catching—or even stopping—one idiot doesn't do a bit of good if you've got a dozen others out there just waiting for their shot to attack the ranch."

"The only saving grace is that time is running out—"

"Which only means the wanna-be heirs are now desperate," Hunter warned. "If you think the snakes were nasty, just wait—"

"I forgot to ask if you wanted cream and sugar," Katherine began as she breezed into the room without warning. Stopping in her tracks at the sight of the two of them with their heads together, she frowned. "What's going on? What'd I miss?"

"We were just discussing the snakes and the possibility of more being in the house," John fibbed quietly, thanking her for the coffee she held out to him. "I know Elizabeth is sleeping, but I didn't want her to hear us talking."

"She's been through enough," Katherine said. "When I pulled back the covers and saw that snake, I thought I was a dead woman."

"You're safe now," Hunter promised huskily, slipping an arm around her. "I'll make sure of it." Glancing back at his brother, he said, "It's late. We need to find a hotel room. I'll have my cell on. Call if you need anything."

Dawn was only a few hours away when Hunter pulled out of the hospital parking lot and went in search of a hotel. Beside him in the cab of John's truck, Katherine was quiet and pensive. Frowning, he shot her a quick glance. "Are you all right?"

Her gaze trained unblinkingly on the road in front of them, she shrugged. "I don't know. I've been thinking a lot about Priscilla and her accident."

"Buck will be there soon. He'll call as soon as he knows something."

"I know. And I have to believe she's going to be all right. But the accident keeps nagging at me. She's a good driver."

"Even the best driver can have an accident," he said. "You can blow a tire or lose control on a slick road. It can happen in the blink of an eye. All you have to do is take your eyes off the road to adjust the radio or dial a cell phone—"

"I've told myself all that," she agreed. "But something in my gut tells me her accident was no accident. Especially after everything that happened at the ranch tonight."

Playing devil's advocate, he said, "The timing could just be a coincidence."

In the darkness she shot him a sharp look. "Do you really believe that?"

"I don't believe in coincidence," he said flatly.

"So you don't think Priscilla's accident was an accident. Why didn't you say something?"

"Because I don't have proof," he said simply. "We don't know the circumstances of the accident yet. Until we do, we don't know anything."

"Except that all of us are away from the ranch tonight," she replied, "and it all started with Buck being drawn away by Priscilla's accident. Then Elizabeth was bitten and I was supposed to be, too."

"If you'd been a little slower, you would have been."

"Which is exactly what whoever did this was hoping for—me and Elizabeth in the hospital, Buck in London with Priscilla, and nobody home. Then they could walk right in and take the ranch—if they're the unnamed heir in Hilda's will." Pale, she hugged herself. "They're going to go after me next."

She was scared, and as much as Hunter wanted to tell her she had nothing to worry about, they both knew better. "The next twenty-four hours are, in all likelihood, going to be damn difficult," he said honestly. "Whoever planted those snakes is going to be closing in for the kill and will pull out all the stops to keep you away from the ranch tomorrow night. We've got to be ready for anything."

"I know."

Her voice was husky, her eyes stark with fear in the glow of the truck's dash lights. Hunter wanted to reach for her, to hold her in his arms until she felt safe, but letting her go when he touched her was becoming more and more difficult for him. Still, he couldn't stand to see her afraid.

"I'll keep you safe," he promised. "I'm not going to

let anyone hurt you. If you want to go home, we'll tear the house apart until you're satisfied it's snake-free. I'll stay up the rest of the night, watching over you while you sleep. All you have to do is say the word—"

For a moment he thought she was going to say yes, but the fear never left her eyes. Finally she shook her head. "No, I can't. Not tonight. Not until daylight."

"Okay," he said easily. "A hotel it is."

Thirty miles away in the small town of Red Bluff, Elliot Fletcher could barely contain his glee as he unlocked the door to his apartment and soundlessly slipped inside. Damn, he felt good! Checking to make sure the door was locked and the curtains closed before he switched on the light, he almost laughed aloud as he saw the thick envelope of money lying on the table by the window. So he'd been paid, just as he'd been promised.

Everything had worked just as he'd planned, he thought in satisfaction. He'd drugged the dogs, then while the family was together at dinner in the dining room, he'd slipped into the cabin, then the house by quietly breaking a window upstairs. He'd never been a second-story man before. He had to admit, breaking in when the family was home had given him a rush he hadn't felt in a long time. And so had leaving the rattlers.

The only thing he regretted was not being able to hide in the house and watch the show when the snakes made their presence known. He might be a risk taker, but he wasn't a fool, and he'd made his escape while he could, loading his ladder into the back of his pickup and driving off without anyone being the wiser. He hadn't, however, gone far…just to the main highway and the thick, dark shadows of a copse of trees just down the road from the ranch entrance. Cutting the engine, he'd pushed the seat back, stretched his legs out and waited in anticipation.

It hadn't taken long. When Buck and his wife had come racing out of the ranch like they were going to a fire, he'd thought they were headed for the hospital. Instead, they'd turned north when they pulled out of the ranch, instead of south, toward Willow Bend. The only thing in that direction was the airport.

Given the chance, he would have followed them just to see where the hell they were going. But he couldn't take the chance. Traffic at that time of night was almost nonexistent, and he couldn't risk drawing attention to himself. So he'd waited, wondering where they could be off to in such a rush.

He'd had plenty of time to speculate about it—hours, in fact. He'd expected some response to the snakes by eleven o'clock, midnight at the latest. Instead, the hours had ticked by and still there'd been no sign of the rest of the Wyatts. Then, just when he'd begun to wonder if he'd once again screwed up, he'd seen a vehicle racing down the ranch's driveway toward the main gate. Just before it reached the gate, it stopped and the dome light was switched on, revealing the two Wyatt women and Hunter and John in the extended-cab pickup.

Hardly giving the men a second glance, he'd studied the women in the harsh light of the truck's overhead light, and there'd been no question that they were both pale and upset. Katherine had even looked as if she'd been crying.

For a moment he'd almost felt sorry for her. He'd enjoyed the time he spent with her—she was fun and interesting—and if things had been different, he'd have made a serious play for her just for the hell of it. But he didn't have time for a woman, especially one who stood in the way of more money than he'd ever made in a single heist.

He'd done what he was paid to do, he told himself. If Katherine and her sister spent a few days in the hospital, he couldn't be concerned about that. When a man made a deal with the devil, he had no other choice but to follow through on his end of the bargain.

It was over, thank God, he thought with a sigh of relief as he headed for the bathroom for a shower before going to bed. And tonight, he thought with a grin, he was going to sleep like a baby. It was payday, and the bastard who'd hired him no longer had a reason to come after him.

His thoughts on what he was going to do with the money, he stepped into the shower and let the hot water stream over him. Maybe he'd go to Vegas and see if he could double his money, he mused. He was feeling lucky.

Ten minutes later, he hit the light switch, shrouding the apartment in darkness, and crawled into bed. As he stretched out in the dark, he never saw the coral snake under his pillow. Before he quite realized he wasn't alone in the bed, it bit him in the jugular vein.

Thirty minutes later, the front door of the apartment opened soundlessly. The visitor who stepped into the darkness quietly shut the door, then carefully set down the cage that had been brought for the snake. When the light was switched on, Elliot Fletcher was still alive. He was, however, in no condition to cause any problems. The snake had gotten him in the throat, and the venom was quickly racing toward his heart. Lying on the floor, where he'd obviously fallen when he'd tried to summon help, the poor fool had been wasting his time and only shortening his life. There was no phone in the apartment—that had been removed when the money was dropped off—and there was no one in the apartments on either side of Fletcher's to hear his weak calls. He was doomed.

"H-help me."

His pitiful cry little more than a whisper, his breathing shallow and ragged, he was drooling like a mad dog and seemed to have no idea that it was too late for help. His fate was sealed—he would die alone in a seedy apartment, and no one would have a clue how a coral snake had not only gotten into his apartment and bitten him, but also gotten out. No witnesses saw his visitor park three blocks away and walk in the dark to the run-down apartment he called home. There were no fingerprints, no tire prints, no evidence left anywhere to indicate that Fletcher had even had a visitor. When his death was investigated, there was only one conclusion the medical examiner would be able come to…he'd died of a snakebite.

"Sorry," the visitor said coldly. "I'm not a doctor."

Fletcher gurgled something unintelligible, then finally went still. Stepping over him, the visitor carefully searched the room for the snake and found it curled up under the bed. Once the bed was carefully pulled away from the wall, the snake was easily snared and secured in the carrier.

"Oh, yes," the visitor told the now still Fletcher. "I forgot the little package of money I left earlier. I hope you don't mind, but I'm going to take it with me. After all, it's not like you're going to need it."

"No."

"You're in no position to argue, you poor fool," the visitor retorted as the money was stored in a pocket. "Nice doing business with you."

Picking up the cage holding the snake, the visitor quietly opened the door, then checked to make sure all was quiet outside before stepping out of the apartment and shutting the door. Without a backward look at the man dying on the floor, the visitor disappeared into the night.

The sleepy desk clerk gave Hunter and Katherine a hostile look. "You're joking, right? You really want a room at four o'clock in the morning? Are you crazy?"

"No, we're tired," Hunter growled, "and we don't feel like driving all the way home tonight. Are you going to give us a room or not?"

"Don't get testy with me, mister," he retorted. "There's a gun show in town and I've got the only room left in town. Push me, and you can go sleep in your car for all I care."

Biting his tongue, Hunter almost told him to go to hell, but Katherine wasn't ready to face the snakes at home, and he'd be damned if he'd make her sleep in the truck. Drawing in a calming breath, he said with exaggerated politeness, "Let's start over, shall we? We need a room. We'll take whatever you've got."

Without a word, the clerk pushed a registration card across the counter. "That'll be ninety-eight dollars."

Katherine gasped. "Are you serious? It's—"

"We'll take it," Hunter cut in. Hurriedly filling out the registration card, he pulled out his wallet and slid a credit card across the desk. Five minutes later, armed with the room key and fresh towels that were so thin you could practically see through them, he opened the door to their room and motioned for her to precede him inside.

Stepping across the threshold, Katherine reached blindly for the light switch. The second the lights came on, she stopped dead in her tracks at the sight of the bed. There was only one.

Following her inside, Hunter followed her gaze to the bed and swore. "Damn! I just assumed there'd be two beds. I'm sorry, Katherine. Look, you take the bed. I'll stretch out on the floor."

"Don't be ridiculous," she said, shaking off her surprise. "I just wasn't expecting—" Heat climbing in cheeks, she forced a grimace of a smile. "I didn't mean to be a baby. It's a king-size bed and we're both exhausted. There's absolutely no reason why we can't share it." And not giving him a chance to argue further, she kicked off her shoes and stretched out on top of the bedspread.

Hunter hesitated. Every instinct he had urged him to forget the bed, forget the floor and sit up all night. It would have been the smart thing to do. But, damn, he was tired! And she was right. It was a king-size bed. He'd just stay on his side.

Giving in, he moved to the opposite side of the bed and lay down with a soundless groan. There was at least four feet of space between them. What was he worried about?

Already half-asleep, he closed his eyes...and felt Katherine move beside him. A few minutes later he was just seconds away from slipping into complete unconsciousness when she shifted beside him, then moved again. Just when he thought she'd settled into a more comfortable position, she punched her pillow and swore under her breath. His eyes still closed, he growled, "What's wrong?"

"I guess I'm too tired," she sighed, sitting up. "I'm exhausted, but I can't seem to turn my brain off. I keep thinking about Priscilla's accident...and the snakes."

Even in the darkness that was broken by the outside security light that peeked between the drapes covering the window, he could see her shiver. "You're safe, Kitty-Kat," he said huskily. "I'm not going to let anyone hurt you."

"I know. And I'm not usually a scaredy—"

Suddenly realizing what she was about to say, she stopped, but she might as well have saved herself the trouble. "Go ahead and say it," he chuckled. "Scaredy-cat. Not that you are one," he added, sobering. "Even if you were, who could blame you? My God, you practically shook hands with a rattler and managed to escape without a scratch. If I were you, I wouldn't be able to sleep, either."

"I know, but I'm keeping you awake."

"I'm fine."

"Well, I'm not! I can't relax. I feel like I'm coming apart at the seams. This is crazy—what are you doing?"

Sitting up behind her, Hunter settled his hands on her shoulders and began to work the tension out of her tight muscles. "Helping you relax," he said simply. "Just close your eyes and turn your brain off."

He made it sound so easy, she thought with a silent groan as he massaged a particularly sensitive spot on the back of her neck. But how was she supposed to relax when the feel of his hands set her heart pounding? When his hands moved slowly over her and her breath seemed to catch in her lungs? When she suddenly found herself remembering his kisses, the taste of his mouth on hers, she knew she was in trouble.

She should have told him a massage wasn't smart right now. Her emotions were on a roller coaster, and all she wanted to do was curl into his arms. If she did…

Images teased and seduced her…his mouth on hers, lightly, softly, making her forget, making her ache. And his hands. Dear God, they were so sure and strong, so tender. She could almost feel them moving over her, trailing over her breast, up her thigh…

When she sighed as he slid his hands gently down her arms and up again, Hunter felt the soft release of her breath ripple through her and just barely bit back a groan. Too late, he realized he should have kept his hands to himself. They were sharing a bed, for heaven's sake. Okay, so they both were completely dressed and lying on top of the covers. It didn't seem to matter. He really had intended to just help her relax, but touching her was…intoxicating. And he couldn't stop.

Giving in to the need that pulled at him, he leaned forward and gently kissed the back of her neck. He half expected her to pull away. Instead she moaned and seemed to turn boneless in his hands. "Hunter…"

"Shhh," he whispered, trailing his mouth to the curve of her neck and shoulder. "Just listen to the pounding of your heart."

His hands slid over her, making her shudder, then gasp. Later he couldn't say when she turned to him. Suddenly she was in his arms and he couldn't stop kissing her. He reached for the buttons of her shirt, the snap of her jeans, her zipper. Following his lead, her hands were there to pull his shirt over his head, then sweep over his shoulders, his chest, to the snap of his jeans. Kissing him, seducing him, she made him all sorts of promises without saying a word.

"I've dreamed of you like this," he rasped. "It's been driving me crazy."

Surprise bloomed in her eyes. Pulling back, she studied him searchingly. "You dreamed of me?"

Enticed by the half smile that played around her mouth, he traced it with his index fingers. "Mmm-hmm."

"How was I?"

"Hot," he murmured. "Sweet. Wild."

She had never considered herself wild, but when he trailed kisses down her neck and chest, then teased first one nipple, then the other with his tongue, need tightened like a fist deep inside her. Her thoughts blurred, making it impossible for her to think of anything but the ache he stirred in her so effortlessly. Tugging the rest of his clothes off, she cried out as he pulled her down beside him, under him.

After that, all she could think of was the feel of his skin against hers as he moved over her, the heat of his fingers as they stroked and rubbed and drove her crazy. Then his mouth replaced his fingers, and just that easily, he destroyed her.

Chapter 11

Seated at a corner table in the hospital cafeteria, Katherine was just about to take a bite of the cinnamon roll Hunter had bought her for breakfast when her cell phone rang. Lightning quick, she hit the talk button without bothering to check the caller ID. It couldn't be anyone but Buck. "How is she?"

"Not as bad as we first thought," he replied tiredly. "The doctor had to remove her spleen because of the accident, but other than that, she's doing fine. She should be out of here by the end of the week."

"Thank God! I was so worried."

"What about Elizabeth?" he growled. "I got a message from John that Elizabeth's in the hospital—but his cell phone went straight to voice mail when I called him back. What the hell's going on? She was fine when we left yesterday. Is she sick?"

"She was bitten by a rattlesnake."

"What?"

"Someone planted rattlesnakes in my bed and Elizabeth's."

"Bloody hell! Are you all right? How is Lizzie?"

"I'm fine," she said, shivering at the memory of the rattler in her own bed. "I jumped back before the snake could get me. Lizzie wasn't so lucky. It bit her on the hand."

He swore. "What does the doctor say?"

"There'll be some tissue damage. And she was horribly sick, of course, but she's going to be fine. Hunter and I stopped by to see her just a few minutes ago, but she and John were both asleep. It was a rough night."

"It sounds like a nightmare," he growled. "When's she coming home?"

"It'll be at least three days. She's been through hell. Hunter said not as many people die from rattlesnake bites as you might think, but she had a horrible reaction to the venom. If we hadn't got her to the hospital when we did, I think she would have been in serious trouble."

"How the hell did someone get in the house with snakes?" he demanded. "This is ludicrous!"

"That's what Hunter and I are trying to figure out," she said. "We haven't been back to the house—we stayed at the Pine Cone Inn after we were sure Elizabeth was all right—but we're going to check the surveillance films as soon as we get home."

"You know whoever did this will be coming after you, don't you?" he said grimly. "I'm not trying to scare you, but you really need to be careful, sis. We've all been gone one night already. All it takes is one more…"

"I know," she said quietly. "But I'm not going to lose the ranch, Buck. If that means I have to sleep in a tent in the middle of a pasture, then I will. And Hunter's with me," she added. "Trust me, he's just as determined as the rest of us to get his hands on whoever planted those snakes."

"What's he got planned for tonight? Let me talk to him."

Seated across the table from Hunter, she handed him the phone. "Buck's worried about tonight."

"He's not the only one," he said dryly as he took the cell phone from her. "Hey, Buck. How's Priscilla?"

"Better than Elizabeth, apparently," he retorted. "What's your strategy for tonight?"

"To batten down the hatches and prepare for whatever these jackasses throw at us."

"I assume John's going to spend the night at the hospital with Elizabeth?"

"He's not leaving her side," he said. "I can't say I blame him. Last night was a nightmare for her and Katherine."

"You probably should stop by the sheriff's office on the way out of town and let him know what's going on," Buck recommended. "Don't wait until you're in trouble before you call for help."

"I won't," he promised. "I'll take good care of Katherine, Buck. I won't tell you not to worry—I know you will—but if anyone tries to hurt her, they're going to have to go through me first."

"I appreciate that," he said huskily. "Rainey and I can't come home until Priscilla's out of the hospital and able to take care of herself. That could be a week or more."

"I'll keep you posted on what's going on. And

tomorrow morning I'll call you the second the sun comes up."

Hanging up, he handed the phone to Katherine, only to curl his fingers around hers when she reached for it. "He's worried about you."

"I am, too," she admitted as her fingers automatically gripped his. But it wasn't the coming night that had her heart pounding. It was Hunter...and their lovemaking. She tried to tell herself that it was just sex, but what she and Hunter had shared wasn't even remotely close to that. And that scared the hell out of her. He wasn't the kind of man who seemed the least bit interested in commitment. Once he helped catch whoever was threatening her family and the ranch, he would move on to God knew where and not look back. She wouldn't be standing on the front porch with tears in her eyes watching him leave. She wouldn't be able to bear it.

"Hey, Kitty-Kat, where'd you go? You're daydreaming about me, aren't you? C'mon, sweetheart, you can admit it. I can see it in your eyes."

Coming back to her surroundings with a blink, she arched a brow. "You think so, do you? And you call yourself a private investigator. Imagine that."

Grinning, he slapped his hand over his heart and groaned, "God, I love it when you tease me! Do it again."

"I don't think so," she laughed.

"Tease."

"Flirt."

"Guilty as charged."

Her heart pounding as his foot rubbed against hers under the table, she found herself aching for his touch.

For no other reason than that, it was time to go. Gathering her purse, she retorted, "Be that as it may, we don't have time to sit around all day and flirt. In case you've forgotten, we've got to get back to the ranch and get ready for tonight."

"Let's go," he said. "We've got a couple of stops to make first, though. Buck suggested we stop by the sheriff's office. We need to report the snakes and let the authorities know what's going on tonight."

"It won't do any good," she said as they headed for Buck's truck, "but I agree. If we need the sheriff tonight, we may not have time to explain why."

"What do you mean...someone planted snakes in the house and the foreman's cabin?" Seated with his feet propped on his desk and crossed at the ankle, Sheriff Clark scowled at the two of them as if they were speaking a foreign language. "How do you know that?"

Hunter just barely stopped himself from rolling his eyes. "Because there were two snakes in two different beds in two different houses on the ranch. What do you think the odds are of that happening without some help from a human being, Sheriff?"

"We don't work on odds here, son," the older man retorted, taking exception to his tone. "But I see your point. I thought Buck had security cameras installed."

Hunter didn't have to ask him how he knew that—they'd bought the cameras right there in town. Not surprisingly the news had, apparently, spread like wildfire. "We haven't had a chance to check the film yet, since we spent what was left of the night here in town. We'll check it as soon as we get home, but in the meantime,

I wanted to let you know what was going on in case we need help tonight. We can count on your men if we need them, can't we?"

"Absolutely," he said promptly.

"And you or one of your deputies will come immediately?" Katherine pressed. "We can count on you to be there for us and not leave us blowing in the wind?"

"Of course," he said, narrowing his eyes at her. "I don't appreciate you implying that my men don't do their duty, Miss Wyatt. In case you haven't noticed, this is a small office—I only have so many deputies to go around. Sometime we're spread a little thin. But if at all possible, we will get to you immediately if you need our services."

"That's why we're here, Sheriff Clark," she said sweetly, too sweetly. "To inform you that we *will* need your services at some point tonight."

"And if you can't make it out to the ranch when we call," Hunter added smoothly, "then we'll have to take matters into our hands. We will be armed and ready. If someone tries to break in or attack us, we have the law behind us if we shoot them, don't we, Sheriff? We do have the right to protect ourselves?"

"Yes, you do," he retorted. "But I'd be careful waving a gun around if I were you, if you don't know what you're doing."

"Oh, *I* know exactly what I'm doing," he assured him coolly. "And don't worry. If we do have to shoot someone, there'll be no question that it's self-defense." His point made, Hunter turned on his heel and headed for the door. "C'mon, Katherine. We've got some ammo to buy."

Hurrying after him, she frowned as she caught up with him outside. "Why are we buying ammunition?

The gun cabinet in Buck's office has enough guns and bullets for an army."

"I know," he chuckled as he opened the passenger door for her, "but no one but the family knows that. I want to make sure the entire town knows we've got enough firepower to take on Butch Cassidy and his gang if we need to. And trust me, when we walk out of the gun shop loaded for bear, the word will get out."

He was right. An hour later when Hunter paid the bill for the guns and ammunition he'd bought and they carried everything out to the truck, it seemed like everyone in Willow Bend was within sight of the gun shop. And Katherine never knew how it happened. She didn't see anyone in the shop call anyone, but suddenly half a dozen potential costumers pulled into the parking lot. At the hardware store across the street, several different contractors who were in the process of loading their trucks with building materials stopped what they were doing to turn and watch their every move.

"Well, we certainly got everyone's attention," she said wryly as they climbed into the truck and headed down Main Street. "What do you want to bet the phone lines are buzzing right about now?"

"They're probably overloaded," he said with a chuckle. "Good. The more people who know the kind of firepower we're packing, the better. Only a fool would come after you knowing they could get his head blown off. Of course," he added, "there are a lot of fools out there. In my business, I run into them all the time. They all think they're smarter than everyone else, cagier, more conniving, when they're generally dumb as a post."

"So you think someone will still attack the ranch tonight?"

"Oh, yeah," he retorted. "But this time we're going to be ready for them."

"First, we take care of the snakes," she said flatly. "I'm not going through that again."

"That's first on our list," he promised. "We'll search the house from top to bottom."

Katherine's stomach turned over at the thought of once again coming face-to-face with a snake. "You think we'll find anything?"

"We've got plenty of ammunition if we do," he said wryly, "so don't worry. This time at least we're prepared. And trust me, you won't be sticking your hand anywhere a snake might be hiding. There are some canes in the umbrella stand in the front hall. We'll use those."

Two hours and one snake later, Katherine was able to walk through the house without skirting around every piece of furniture in the place. They'd searched under every bed, chair, table, couch and cabinet in the house, as well as all the closets and cupboards and behind the drapes and curtains. When they searched the closet in Buck and Rainey's room, they heard the rattler long before Hunter pulled back the hanging dresses at one end of the closet.

Katherine hadn't panicked, though her heart had slammed against her ribs, and before she could stop herself, she'd taken three quick steps back. Hunter, however, had stood his ground and pulled out a pistol. A split second later, the snake was dead.

After that, it soon became apparent that whoever

had planted the snakes had placed one in each of the Wyatts' beds. The rest of the house was clean. There was, however, no time to relax. They had to check the surveillance tapes. It shouldn't take more than ten minutes for them to discover who had cold-bloodedly tried to kill every member of the family.

But when Hunter sat down at the computer in Buck's office and pulled up the tapes, there was no sign of an intruder anywhere.

"Son of a bitch!" Hunter swore. "Did he get to the tapes and erase them?"

"He couldn't have," Katherine said, frowning at the monitor as Hunter replayed the pictures taken from each of the cameras set up at every corner of the house. "Everyone was here but us. Surely Buck or John would have noticed someone slipping into the office."

"Then give me another explanation," he retorted, "because this doesn't make a damn bit of sense...unless the snakes were brought into the house before the cameras were put up. And I don't think there would have been time. We were all here. Hell, even your boyfriend and the sheriff were here!"

Her eyes locked on the monitor, Katherine hardly heard him. "Wait a minute," she said with a frown. "Run the tapes of the east end of the house again."

"Why? Did you see something?"

"No. That's the problem. Where's the tree by the kitchen? You know, the one that's right up against the house?"

"What do you mean? It's right where it's always been—"

Breaking off abruptly, he scowled, and immediately punched the keys that brought up a different angle of the same scene. There still was no sign of the tree. "Son of a—"

"It's a blind spot," she said, surprised. "The cameras are pointed down, toward the windows."

"The *downstairs* windows," he corrected her, swearing, "and there isn't one by the tree."

"There is upstairs," she told him. "It's at the end of the hallway."

"So, what are you saying? Someone broke in upstairs?"

"It wouldn't be difficult if they had a ladder...and a blind spot."

He hadn't even considered that. Feeling like a fool, he swore roundly. "Dammit! You're right! I didn't even think of that. Once word got out about the cameras, all anyone had to do was check the direction the security lights were angled, figure out the blind spots and find a way inside. All they needed was a damn ladder." Pushing back from the desk, he said, "C'mon. Let's go check the window."

They hurried upstairs to check the window, and neither one of them was surprised when they discovered that one of the panes had been cut and removed so the intruder could unlock the window and slip inside. "Well, that explains that," he said in disgust. "What do you want to bet that the perp wore gloves? So we've got no pictures, no fingerprints. We're right back where we started."

"Except that we know there's bound to be an attack tonight and we don't know where it's coming from," she said.

"Don't worry," he said. "We'll be ready."

"So what do we first?"

"Round up the cattle."

Stunned, she looked at him wide-eyed. "You're joking, right?"

"I've never been more serious in my life," he said flatly. "C'mon."

Taking her hand, he led her out to the barn and saddled horses for both of them. It was only as they were about to mount up that Katherine saw the dogs lying unmoving on the ground in their pen. "Oh, my God! Are they dead?"

"No, just knocked out," Hunter said grimly as he checked them. "My guess is whoever put the snake in your bed gave them sleeping pills."

"What kind of monster would do that? What will he do next?"

"Don't go there," he growled, crossing to wrap her in his arms. "We can only deal with one crisis at a time. Right now, we've gotr cows to round up."

"But what about the dogs?"

"They'll have to sleep it off." Helping her into her saddle, he then mounted his own horse. "Let's go," he said, and touched his heels to his horse. Seconds later they were racing toward the cattle in the pasture a half mile from the house.

"You've lost your mind. Elizabeth's going to kill us if her rosebushes get trampled."

"She's not going to get the chance if someone else gets to us first," he retorted.

"And cows in the front yard are going to keep us safe?"

Hunter grinned. "Oh, we're not going to corral them

just in the front yard—they're going to be all around the house."

"What? Why?"

"Because tonight is the dark of the moon," he explained. "With no moon, it'll be as dark as pitch and the cows won't be in their usual pasture. They'll be as anxious as a bunch of kids afraid of the dark. If anyone even thinks about coming around, they're going to let us know."

"You sure? Cows really do that?"

"They get nervous," he said simply. "When they do, we'll be ready. As soon as we're finished here, we've got a hell of a lot of ammunition to set up."

"Define *finish*," she said with a frown.

He grinned. "We need more cows."

By the time the sun started to sink below the mountains to the west, they were ready for just about anything. Two hundred cows were confined within the fence that surrounded the homestead compound, all downstairs doors were locked and barricaded, and the interior shutters on the windows were also shut and barred. Without a battering ram—or a bazooka—no one was getting into the house.

As twilight deepened and Katherine headed upstairs with Hunter on her heels, her nerves were jumpy, her stomach in knots. She tried to convince herself that she and Hunter were as safe as they could possibly be, but her common sense wasn't buying it. How could they be safe when they didn't know who was after them or what direction the attack would come from? There were shotguns and rifles at every upstairs window, but what if whoever was determined to drive them away from the ranch came in a tank? It wasn't likely, but at this point, she couldn't be sure of anything.

Suddenly cold, she found herself hugging herself as they reached the top of the stairs. "Now what?" she said huskily. "Do we just pick a window and wait?"

"We'll get to that," he told her. "First, I want you to change into something black—preferably pants and a long-sleeved shirt."

"It's summer, Hunter," she reminded him. "I didn't bring any long-sleeved clothes with me."

"Then borrow something," he told her. "I'll meet you in the upstairs family room as soon as you're ready."

"Give me five minutes," she told him and hurried into Buck and Rainey's room to search through their closets. Neither of them wore black on a regular basis, so she had to dig to the back of the closet before she found an old pair of faded jeans that belonged to Rainey and a navy-blue shirt that she'd given to Buck two Christmases ago and had never seen him wear. Now she knew what happened to it!

Grinning at the thought, she quickly changed, then hurried into the family room to find Hunter already there, waiting for her in the growing twilight. He hadn't turned any lights on, and in the thickening shadows, he, too, was dressed in black and looked dark and dangerous. Katherine took one look at him and found her thoughts drifting to the hours they'd spent at the motel, the taste of him, the feel of him, the *heat* of him—

"Ready?"

His husky voice slid over her like a caress, setting her pulse throbbing, distracting her... Suddenly realizing he'd said something, she frowned. "What?"

He only laughed—and lightly rubbed his fingers across her cheek. It was only when he grinned down at her and she caught a glimpse of the wicked mischief in his eyes that she realized he'd wiped something on her face. "What did you do?"

"Just putting a little mud on your face, sweetheart," he said innocently.

"Hunter!"

"Your skin's so pale," he said, chuckling when she rubbed her hand across cheek and wiped some of the mud off, then transferred it to his face. Lightning quick, he grabbed her hand and stuck her fingers in a bowl of mud she hadn't even seen in his hands. "There you go, Kitty-Kat. Take as much as you want and rub it all over me if you want. I don't mind at all. Then if anyone's out there, watching the house, they won't be able to see us."

Brought back to their situation with those simple words, she felt her heart stop dead in her breast. "Do you really think we can be seen from the windows?"

"I'm not taking any chances," he said simply, and dipped his fingers in the bowl of mud. Two seconds later, he dropped a big glob on her nose.

He would have loved to strip her bare and wipe the mud all over her and have her do the same to him, but it would soon be completely dark. Like it or not, it was time to get back to the business at hand.

Suddenly serious, he gently spread the mud on her nose across her cheeks. "Okay, sweetheart, no more teasing. It's going to be showtime here in a little while and we've got to be prepared."

Sobering, she nodded. "I know. What do you want me to do?"

"Take up a position at the window here in the family room. I'll be right across the hall in your room, keeping an eye on the back of the house."

"What if the attack comes from the side of the house?"

"I'll keep watch out the side windows, too," he assured her. "You just stay here and watch the cows. The lights will be out, so once your eyes adjust to the darkness, you'll be able to see more than you think you will. Watch the cows now, see how they graze around the house, then you'll be able to notice a change in them the second our *friends* show up. And if you need me, scream bloody hell if you have to. Okay?"

Her heart in her throat, she nodded. "What happens when they get here? What do we do then?"

"Play it by ear," he said simply. "Your guns are loaded—all you have to do is point and shoot. Don't worry if you hit anything in the dark. The objective is to scare them off. It that doesn't work, all we can do is hope like hell we're prepared for whatever they throw at us." Pulling her into his arms for a hug, he kissed her in the growing darkness. "Try not to be afraid," he said huskily. "I'm not going to let anything happen to you."

She didn't doubt for a minute that he would do everything within his power to protect her, but as she settled at the open window with a pair of high-powered binoculars and a loaded shotgun and rifle at her side, he wasn't the one she was worried about. It was the unknown "friends" out there in the darkness who had already proved that they would do just about anything to get their hands on the ranch.

Wide-awake at eleven o'clock and stiff from sitting in one place too long, Katherine pushed to her feet and was just about to find her way to the bathroom in the dark when she heard several of the cows moo in the darkness. Her heart suddenly pounding, she turned back to the window and peered out at the cows in the front yard. Were they moving more than they had been? Or was it just her imagination that they seemed restless?

"Hunter? I think something's going on!"

Even to her own ears, her voice was high-pitched and full of panic, but she couldn't help it. It was the unknown that scared her to death, the not knowing where or from whom the attack was going to come that terrified her to death. They were dealing with desperate, crazy people who didn't seem to have a scruple between them. What if—

"Did you see something?"

Startled, she jumped at Hunter's quiet question as he suddenly appeared beside her in the dark. She hadn't even heard him step into the room. "Don't do that! You scared me!"

"Sorry," he said, chuckling, only to quickly sober as he looked out the window. "The cows aren't happy about something."

"I know. For the last ten minutes, they've been milling about anxiously."

Suddenly, with no warning, a window shattered in one of the bedrooms at the far end of the hall. Swearing,

Hunter grabbed a gun and thrust it into her hands, then snatched up another one for himself. "C'mon!"

Bursting out of the room, he started to run down the hall, but he'd only taken a few steps when another window shattered, this time at the opposite end of the hall. Almost immediately they both smelled smoke.

"Oh, God!" Katherine gasped. "The house is on fire."

"Not on fire," Hunter growled, swearing. "It's a smoke bomb. See, there are no flames. Dammit to hell, they're going to smoke us out! Quick, grab a pillowcase and fill it with as much ammunition as you can carry. We've got to get the hell out of here!"

Her heart in her throat, she jerked open the door to the linen closet and blindly grabbed some pillowcases from the middle shelf. Seconds later she sprinted back into the family room and started wildly throwing ammunition into the cases.

She never saw the smoke bomb that was hurtled toward the window directly behind her. Suddenly, shattered glass rained down on her head, and the smoke bomb hit her hard on the shoulder, then landed on the floor beside her. She gasped...and just that quickly, she was choking.

Chapter 12

Swearing, Hunter grabbed Katherine around the waist and hauled her through the smoke into the hall. "Run!" he barked, and jerked his phone out of his pocket to call the sheriff. "Someone's throwing smoke bombs into the Wyatt homestead!" he barked into the phone. "We're under attack. Get someone the hell out here!"

Not waiting for an answer, he hung up and pulled Katherine toward the stairs. The house was pitch-black, and even though Hunter knew where every step was, he found himself nearly stumbling on the stairs in the dark. Swearing, he slipped an arm around Katherine's waist as they made their way, coughing, to the first floor.

"We can't hide in here any longer—the smoke's getting worse," he told her hoarsely. "We're going to have to make a run for it."

"But what about whoever threw the smoke bombs?" she choked out, alarmed. "Won't they be waiting for us?"

"They won't be able see us," he promised. "And unless they've got guards set up at every door and window, they're not going to have a clue which one we're coming out of unless they're standing right in front of us. While they're still looking for us, we'll be hiding out in the barn."

Pulling her with him into Buck's office, he cautiously opened the shutters and looked outside. The night was dark, quiet, too still except for the restless movements of the cattle. Casting a quick glance at Katherine, who stood like a dark shadow beside him, he said huskily, "Ready?"

No! she wanted to cry. Smoke might be billowing down the stairs, chasing them, but at least they were protected to some degree from the monsters outside who could be waiting with rifles to pick them off like sitting ducks the second they stepped outside. "They could have lights," she said worriedly. "We won't have a chance—"

"Sweetheart, we don't have a chance if we stay here. We've got to get out of here!"

The smoke from the stairs came racing toward them, and just that quickly, they ran out of time. Giving her a quick hug, he released her to unlock and open a window. Smoke billowed around them, escaping through the window and giving away their position to anyone with sharp enough night vision to see the smoke in the dark.

Swearing, he quickly stepped through the window and set the guns and ammunition on the ground next to him before turning to help Katherine out the window. When she immediately started toward the barn, he pulled her quickly back against him. "Wait," he said in a soundless whisper, and glanced sharply to the left and right to make sure the coast was clear. Between where they stood, pressed against the house, and the barn, all he saw was the black shadows that were the cows as they milled about, grazing on Elizabeth's rose garden.

"Now," he said gruffly in her ear and pushed her toward the barn.

They ran like the hounds of hell were after them, crouching low as they used the cows for cover. But they'd barely taken four steps when a shot rang out. A split second later, a bullet plowed into the ground, kicking up dirt just inches from Hunter's feet. Swearing, he darted around a tree just as Katherine dodged around the one closest to her.

Another shot rang out.

At the sound of Katherine's startled cry of pain, Hunter's heart stopped dead in his chest. "Katherine!"

"I'm all right," she gasped, only to cry out again as another shot rang out. "It missed me—"

Livid, Hunter sprinted around the tree—and the cows that were suddenly blocking his path—and reached Katherine just as their assailant fired again. This time, however, they were two steps from the barn. Swearing, he grabbed her and jerked her into the barn just as a bullet slammed into the side of the barn.

The dark inside was complete and all-consuming. So furious he could almost feel steam pouring out of his ears, Hunter turned to her immediately. "Where were you hit?" he demanded hoarsely, running his hands quickly over her. "Did they only get you once? Dammit, Katherine, say something!"

"I'm trying to," she said. "The bullet just nicked my arm. I'm all right. Really."

Hunter wanted to believe her, but when he found the wound on the back of her arm and pulled his hands back, his fingers were dripping with blood. "That's not a damn nick," he growled, jerking a handkerchief out of his pocket and tying it around her arm. "We've got to get you to the hospital!"

"It's not serious," she insisted. "And even if it was, we're trapped here, in case you hadn't noticed. We can't just walk out—"

"The hell we can't!" Furious that she was bleeding and there wasn't a damn thing he could do about it except tie a makeshift bandage around it, he grabbed a rifle and fired six shots out into the darkness, then reloaded and fired again.

In the silence of the night, his shots echoed eerily, then died away. He wanted to believe at least one of his bullets had found their assailant, but even the strongest man couldn't take a hit from a .22 without a yelp of pain. The jackass was still out there, hiding in the night. What would he do next?

"Where the hell's the sheriff?" he growled. "He and his men should have been here by now. They were warned this was going to happen."

"I'm sure they're on their way," Katherine said quietly. "Maybe they got another call—"

"To hell with that," he retorted. "I'll bet the last time this county had any major problems with crime, Truman was in office."

"I'm not dying, Hunter."

"No, you're just bleeding, dammit, and I don't like it. I'm going to get the truck—"

"No!"

"It's parked in the lean-to attached to the barn," he argued. "I can pull it right up to the door."

"And chance getting shot, too? No! It's too dangerous—"

Suddenly, in the tense silence of the night, the sound of approaching sirens echoed eerily in the distance. And their attacker heard it at the same time they did. A muttered curse was uttered in the all-consuming darkness, then the thud of running feet.

Hunter swore and started to take off after him when he remembered Katherine. For all he knew, their assailant could be hiding behind a tree, waiting for him to run past so that he could dispose of him, then come back for Katherine before the sheriff arrived. It wouldn't take long—only a few minutes—then he could kidnap Katherine and hold her captive until dawn. That's all it would take, and the fight to keep the ranch would all be over.

"Aren't you going after him?"

In the darkness, he could just make her out standing in the doorway, frowning at him. "No," he said grimly as he joined her. "It could be a setup. I won't chance leaving you alone. How's your arm?"

"I'm all right."

"Katherine—"

"It burns a little," she admitted. "I'm sure I'll be fine."

"I'd rather hear that from a doctor—"

The scream of the approaching sirens grew increasingly loud until suddenly, two county patrol cars raced down the drive and into the ranch compound. Fifty feet behind them were two ambulances and a fire truck.

"Well, it's about damn time," Hunter said, relieved.

"It looks like they sent the cavalry. Over here!" he called out to the EMTs, hitting the light switch just inside the barn to flood it and the surrounding yard with lights. "Katherine's been shot!"

The words weren't even out of his mouth when Katherine was swarmed by the EMTs, who immediately began examining the bloody handkerchief Hunter had tied around her arm in the dark. "I'm all right," she assured them quickly. "The bullet just grazed my arm. Please…just send someone after whoever shot me. He ran at the sound of the sirens. He couldn't have gotten far."

"The shots came from over there," Hunter said, nodding toward the trees to the east of the house. "I think there was only one shooter, but I can't be sure. In the darkness, sounds echo. And two smoke bombs were thrown into the house from different directions. One person could have done it—but so could two."

Sheriff Clark nodded in the direction the shooter had run. "Check it out," he told his men.

"Let me get the lights for you," Hunter said, and strode over to the house to unlock the back door with Katherine's keys. Seconds later the entire compound was flooded with light, and the sheriff and his men were combing over the property like bloodhounds, searching for any evidence the shooter may have left behind.

Rejoining Katherine, Hunter wasn't surprised when the young EMT examining her arm announced, "You really need to go to the hospital for this." In the full light of the floodlights, she was pale and drawn, and if the bloodstains on her clothes were anything to go by, the wound was a heck of a lot more than a "little scratch."

"You can't just bandage it?"

"Sorry, ma'am," he said regretfully. "It's not just a scratch. The bullet actually pierced the fleshy part of your arm, which means a doctor needs to take a look at it. So as soon as we get you loaded in the ambulance, we'll take you in."

"I'll follow in my truck," Hunter told her, squeezing her hand.

"I'm sure I'm fine," she grumbled. "It just seems like a lot of bother over nothing."

"What a baby," he teased. "It's not going to hurt for a doctor to check you out."

She wanted to argue further, but he didn't give her a chance. Spying the sheriff, who'd just walked out of the house after searching it with one of his deputies, he called out, "Are you done with us, Sheriff? Katherine needs to go to the hospital, and I'm going to follow in my truck."

The older man gave him a sharp look. "You sure you want to do that?"

"Katherine doesn't have any choice," he said simply.

"No, I guess she doesn't." His expression grim, he added, "We found the smoke bombs. We'll check them for fingerprints, but I doubt whoever did this made that kind of mistake. We may be able to track down where the bombs were purchased and run a paper trail." He shrugged. "Then again…"

"Don't hold our breaths," Hunter finished for him. "Right?"

To his credit, he didn't lie. "Right."

"If you're finished, Sheriff Clark, we need to go," the EMT cut in smoothly. "We're getting another call on the far side of the county."

"Then you'd better head on out. If you need an escort, just let me know."

Thirty seconds later the ambulance pulled out of the gates of the Broken Arrow Ranch with its emergency lights flashing and siren blaring. By the time it pulled up before the hospital emergency room entrance, the adrenaline that had kept Katherine going since she'd been shot was starting to drop off. Suddenly, the wound was burning as if it was on fire, and at the same time she was chilled to the bone in spite of the fact that she had a blanket covering her. Thankful she was lying down and strapped to the stretcher, she closed her eyes on a moan.

"You all right, Miss Wyatt?" the EMT who was riding in the back of the ambulance asked as he moved to her side to take her pulse.

"No," she groaned, squeezing her eyes shut in an effort to stop her head from its sudden spinning. "I feel awful."

"Let's get your feet up," he said quickly, and elevated the foot of the stretcher. "I'm going to put another blanket over you, but you let me know if you get too warm. We'll have you inside in just a second. Just hang on."

That was easy for him to say when she felt as if she was sliding off the edge of the earth, she thought as they pulled her stretcher out of the ambulance. She just needed something to hang on to…

Even with her eyes shut, she immediately recognized the hand that closed around hers. "What's wrong?" Hunter growled.

"She's going into shock," the young EMT said. "We need to get her inside."

Her head swimming, Katherine tried to hold on to Hunter's hand, but he was forced to release her as they swept her inside. Then the emergency room nurses rushed forward, along with two doctors who didn't look like they were old enough to shave, and her wound was poked and probed and cleaned and stitched. And throughout it all, she told herself she could just endure it if she could just hold Hunter's hand.

She didn't say a word, but somehow he knew. When the doctors finally finished patching her up, Hunter moved to her side and took her hand immediately. In the time it took to blink, her tilting world swung right side up.

"Your room will be ready soon," the doctor said as he stripped off his gloves and tossed them in the trash. "We're going to start you on a round of antibiotics and see how you're doing tomorrow—"

"Oh, no!" Katherine retorted, sitting up. "I'm not staying."

"But—"

"Unless leaving would be dangerous for her, she really has to go home," Hunter said quietly. "She won't be alone, though. I'll keep a close eye on her. What do I need to watch for?"

"Signs of infection," he retorted. "Red streaks coming from the wound, heat, fever, drainage." Frowning at Katherine, he added, "This really isn't wise, Ms. Wyatt. If you insist on leaving, you'll need to sign a release. The hospital can't be held accountable…"

"Of course," she agreed smoothly. "I totally agree. If you'll just get the paperwork, I'll sign it, and Hunter and I will be on our way. We need to get back to the ranch."

Left with no recourse, the young doctor turned on his heel and marched away without another word. Grinning, Hunter said, "Well, I guess you showed him."

"He'll get over it," she said, then suddenly frowned. "Oh, God, I forgot about John and Elizabeth. Do you think we need to tell them about the shooting?"

"No. There's nothing they can do tonight except worry. We'll tell them about it tomorrow. I'm more concerned about you."

"I'm fine."

"You sure? Because I'm telling you right now, if you get home and I think you need a doctor, we're coming right back here and you *will* be spending the night."

She lifted a delicately arched brow at him. "Really? And who gave you the right to boss me around?"

"We'll talk about it when you don't have a bullet hole in your arm," he tossed back. "In the meantime, you're just going to have to trust me to do what's best for you."

A slight smile kicked up one corner of her mouth. "Whether I like it or not?"

"Now you're getting it." Trying and failing to hold on to a frown, he grinned. "I always did like a smart woman."

"Careful, mister," she warned as the nurse brought her release papers and she signed them. "When my arm's better, you're going to pay for that."

"Promises, promises."

"You just wait."

Grinning, he took her left hand and placed it against his heart. "Sweetheart, I've been waiting for you all my life. Don't you know that? C'mon, let's go home."

Her own heart thumping as she sank into the wheel-chair and he pushed her out to his 4Runner, she found herself wondering if he was serious…and if she wanted him to be. The question pulled at her all the way home, but she wouldn't let herself even speculate on an answer. She wasn't ready to go there, didn't want to take a chance on having her heart broken again.

As they approached the ranch entrance, however, she had other worries. "What if whoever was here earlier comes back?"

"Then we call the sheriff again," he retorted. "I'm going to call him anyway to let him know that we're back and will be here the rest of the night."

She paled. "*The rest of the night?* But—"

"We'll be fine," he assured.

"But what about the smoke? It went through the entire house."

"Which is why we're not staying there," he replied. "I thought we'd just stay in the truck. When the back seats are folded down, there's more than enough room for both of us. So where would you like to park? It's your call. I've got four-wheel drive, so we can go anywhere on the ranch you want."

"A pasture where there's not a tree for miles," she said promptly as they reached the house and he braked to a stop in the front drive. "Then we can see anyone sneaking up on us."

"I know just the place," he said promptly. "Give me five seconds to call the sheriff, and we'll go."

While Hunter called the sheriff from the house phone, Katherine collected some blankets from the linen closet to lie on in the 4Runner. A quick check of the dogs assured them they were still sleeping, so they left them where they were and climbed into the truck.

Exhaustion creeping up on her, Katherine leaned her head back against the headrest and closed her eyes as Hunter turned north on one of the many dirt roads that crisscrossed the ranch. For the first time in what seemed like days, she was able to relax. Within minutes the motion of the vehicle lulled her to sleep.

"Katherine?"

Deep in the depths of her dreams, Katherine heard her name whispered on the wind and smiled softly when she recognized Hunter's voice calling to her in the night. A warm fog surrounded her, hiding him from her, but she knew he was close. She could almost hear the pounding of his heart. She was safe. Sighing dreamily, she slipped deeper into unconsciousness.

"C'mon, sweetheart, open those big blue eyes of yours."

His words teased her, pulled at her, tugging her toward wakefulness. Stirring, she frowned slightly. "Hmm?"

"I've got the bed made," he said huskily. "All you have to do is wake up long enough to crawl in the back and slip under the covers. C'mon, I'll help you."

"Where?"

"Into bed," he said with a chuckle. "It's in the back. Remember?"

Confused, she frowned, still unable to open her eyes. "Back of where?"

"The 4Runner, sweetheart," he said, amused. "You wanted to sleep in the middle of a pasture. We're here."

Seeping through the fog of sleep that clouded her

brain, his words suddenly registered, and her eyes flew open with a start. "Hunter?"

Standing in the vee created by the open passenger door and the body of the vehicle, he grinned down at her as he leaned over her. "I'm right here, darlin'."

In the glow of the dome light, he was so close she could see the gold lights of amusement sparkling in his eyes. Drowsy, enchanted, her head spinning just a little, she lifted her hand to his face. "Did I ever tell you you have the most beautiful eyes?"

His grin deepened as he covered her fingers with his. "Those pain pills the doctor gave you must be pretty potent."

Surprise bloomed in her eyes. "I forgot about the pain pills. That must be why I'm so woozy."

"Do you need help getting to the back?"

"Absolutely."

Chuckling, he stepped back and held out his hand. Her heart pounding, she placed her hand in his and let him gently tug her to her feet...and into his arms. It wasn't until he wrapped her close against him that she realized she was right where she wanted to be. Always.

Because she loved him.

The truth came out of nowhere to steal the air right out of her lungs. Still groggy, she tried to deny it. It was the pain pills, she told herself. It had to be. The drugs were clouding her thinking, making her imagine feelings that weren't possible. How could they be? Less than six weeks ago, she'd loved Nigel with all of her heart. Now she couldn't even remember what he looked like.

"Kitty-Kat?"

"Mmm?"

She felt a soft, silent laugh ripple through him. "Sweetheart," he growled, "I thought you wanted to lie down."

"I do."

"Then it looks like it's up to me," he said, smiling as he slipped his arm around her shoulder and guided her around to the back of the vehicle where he already had the rear door open and waiting for her. "In you go. That's it. Just stretch out and close your eyes."

He thought she would fall back asleep the second she was horizontal, but when he crawled in beside her, he'd hardly gotten comfortable next to her when she turned to face him and snuggled up against him. Her head settled on his shoulder, her body pressed against his side, and she buried her face against his neck with a soft sigh.

Just that easily, she sent heat lightning streaking through him and set his body humming. In the time it took to suck in a sharp breath, he wanted her so badly he ached.

His jaw clenching on a groan, he reminded himself that she was hurt. No decent man would take advantage of a woman who had just spent nearly an hour in the emergency room getting a bullet wound cleaned and stitched. She might not be feeling any pain, but that was only because the doctor had given her a shot strong enough to knock out a horse. That could wear off at any time…like when he was kissing her…or undressing her…or sliding into her—

He swore at the thought, but it was too late to stop the images from playing in his head. It was the finest kind of torture. Teased and tormented, he could do nothing but lie there with her pressed close and go quietly out of his mind.

He thought he hid it from her. Then she kissed the side of his neck and ran her fingers slowly down the buttons of his shirt, unbuttoning them one by one. "Kat—"

At his warning tone, the little minx smiled against his neck. "Hmm?"

"You're hurt, remember?"

"I feel fine."

"Your arm—"

"Isn't hurting at all," she assured him. "Those pain pills the doctor gave me really worked."

"You should rest," he rasped, grabbing her hand when her fingers moved to the snap of his jeans. "It's been a rough night."

"This is the best part of it," she murmured, and turned her hand in his. Before he could guess her intentions, she wrapped her fingers around his wrist and cradled his hand to her breast.

Her sigh of pleasure rippled through him like a caress. "You don't play fair," he growled, and kissed her.

Moonlight streamed through the windows of the 4Runner, and from somewhere in the distance, the howl of a wolf floated eerily on the night air. The sound was lonely and wild and echoed in their ears, calling to them in a way they both found impossible to resist.

Need a nagging ache deep inside her, Katherine gave herself up to Hunter's kiss and lost herself in the heat he stirred in her so effortlessly. His clothes disappeared, and then he was undressing her as if she was a present to be unwrapped. His hands moved over her, pulling her clothes from her piece by piece until she was naked, bare, hot with need. Then his fingers lingered… stroked…drove her mad.

Gasping, her blood roaring in her ears, she arched under him, desperate for more, and never remembered calling his name. "Hunter...please..."

"Not yet," he murmured, trailing kisses down her neck, her shoulders, her breasts, wherever his fingers had wandered. "I want to drive you crazy."

"You are!"

His chuckle was soft and seductive in the darkness of the night. "I haven't even begun, sweetheart."

And with no more warning than that, he began a slow, seductive attack on her senses. Any thought she had of prolonging the pleasure went up in smoke with the whisper-soft stroke of his fingers. Then he surged into her, filling her, and she could feel herself coming apart. His groan of satisfaction pushed her over the edge. With a startled cry, she shattered.

The sun was just peeking over the eastern horizon when Katherine stirred in her sleep. Nestled against her back, spoon fashion, Hunter tightened his arm around her waist, holding her close. After their loving, he'd stayed awake all night, making sure she was safe, and still he didn't want to let her go. Not yet. Not ever.

The truth had hit him sometime during the long hours of the night, when he'd stared out at the darkness and felt like they were the only two people on earth. He'd never been more content in his life.

When had he fallen in love with her? How had she managed to slip past his guard? After Sheila's betrayal had nearly cost him his life, he'd sworn that he would never let any woman get close enough to hurt him again. And he hadn't. Until now.

"Good morning."

The soft, velvety purr of her voice stroked him like a caress. Kissing the side of her neck, he growled, "Good morning. How'd you sleep?"

"Wonderfully." Turning in his arms, her smile was slow and sultry as her eyes met his and she pulled him close for a kiss. "How long have you been awake?"

"All night," he said simply.

Surprised, she blinked. "*All night?* Why?"

"I couldn't stop thinking about you," he said simply, pushing her hair back from her face. "I'm falling in love with you."

Whatever she expected him to say, it wasn't that. Sudden tears stinging her eyes, she kissed him softly. "I love you, too."

"You need to know what you're getting into," he said simply, then told her about the secret life he'd led for the CIA, the danger, the only other woman he'd loved, the same one who'd betrayed him and nearly killed him.

"Oh, my God!"

"After I got out of the hospital, I quit my job, changed my name and dropped off the face of the earth," he told her. "I haven't had any problem since, but someone from my past could show up at any time, wanting revenge. I was good at what I did, Katherine. I made enemies."

"Does John know about this?"

He shrugged. "He may suspect, but I never gave him any specifics. All he really knows is that in the past I sometimes used different names and traveled outside the country more than most people. Once I assured him that I wasn't doing anything illegal, he didn't ask any more questions."

"So you're telling me this because...?"

"Because I love you," he said huskily, reaching for her. "After Sheila, I never thought I'd let myself trust another woman enough to love her. Even when I met you, I thought I could handle you. But you challenged me at every step, didn't let me get away with anything, and before I could stop myself, I realized that I loved you."

"Oh, Hunter, I—"

He cut her off with a quick kiss. "No," he said softly, cupping her face in his hands. "Don't say anything. I know how badly Nigel hurt you. What he did was unforgivable, and I wouldn't blame you if you never trusted a man again. But I'm not Nigel. I will never betray you."

"I know that," she said, closing her hands around his wrists as he held her face in his hands. "You're not that kind of man."

"No, I'm not," he agreed. "I love you. I want to marry you, but I'm not going to ask you now. I want you to think about it, to be sure of your feelings. It hasn't been that long since you were in love with Nigel. If you're not over him and need more time, that's all right. We'll deal with it. Okay?"

"I—"

"Just think about it," he said, and kissed her again.

By the time they headed back to the house, noon was only an hour away. They planned to take a shower together and head to the hospital to check on Elizabeth, but they soon discovered she was no longer in the hospital. John was just helping her from a taxi when they arrived at the house. Stunned, Katherine was out of Hunter's 4Runner before he'd even braked to a complete stop.

"What are you doing here?" she demanded as she rushed to her sister's side. "You're still as white as a sheet. You should be in the hospital!"

"I'm fine," Elizabeth assured her, hugging her. "I had to come home and make sure you were all right. A nurse at the hospital told us about the shooting. Are you all right? I tried calling you, but when you didn't answer your phone and John couldn't get Hunter, I was worried something else had happened."

"We were out in one of the north pastures," Hunter explained as his brother paid off the cabdriver and sent him on his way. "I didn't even think to check the phone—we must have been out of range."

"We're both fine," Katherine added. "My arm's sore this morning, but it's just a flesh wound."

"Now that we know everybody's fine, you both need to get somewhere and put your feet up," John said with a frown. "You should be resting, not standing out here in the drive—"

The sound of a car coming up the drive cut through whatever he was going to say next, and the four of them turned just in time to see the sheriff pull up behind Hunter's 4Runner. "Now what?" Elizabeth groaned.

They didn't have to wait long to find out. Stepping from his patrol car, Sherm Clark said, "I was hoping I would find the four of you here. I've got some news."

"Good or bad?" Hunter asked.

"A corpse is never good news."

Katherine and Elizabeth both stiffened. "Who—"

"Elliot Fletcher."

"Who the hell is that?" John demanded. "Never heard of him."

"That's his real name—or the one he used the most," the sheriff said with a grimace. "He also went by Kurt Russell."

Katherine blinked. "What? He's dead? What happened?"

"Snakebite," he retorted. "His apartment manager had to let a repairman into his apartment to fix the air conditioner, and they found him dead. I got a call this morning."

"Oh, my God!"

"Before you start feeling sorry for the jerk, you need to know that I finally got an ID on that print that was found on the jewelry box in your bedroom. It was Russell's...or Fletcher's or Stevens's—he had a hell of a lot of aliases, not to mention a rap sheet as long as my arm. It seems he liked to con women and cheat them out of just about everything they owned."

Katherine wanted to sink right into the ground. "Don't say it," she warned Hunter, but it was too late.

"I told you so."

"He put the snakes in the house, didn't he?" John said. "And drugged the dogs. Then he was bitten himself. It serves him right."

"You're damn straight," Hunter added. "Only a sadistic monster would do what he did. I don't have any sympathy for him."

"When did he die? Do you think he was responsible for the smoke bombs last night and shooting Katherine?"

The sheriff shrugged. "We'll have to wait for the

coroner's report for time of death. In the meantime I'm still checking out those smoke bombs. As soon as I find out something, I'll let you know. Call me if anything else comes up."

"Well, so much for that," Hunter said as they watched the older man drive off. "At least we know who's responsible for the snakes."

"That was my fault," Katherine said. "I'm sorry, Elizabeth. If I hadn't gotten involved with him, you never would have gotten bit."

"Don't beat yourself up over it, sweetheart," Hunter told her. "Even if you hadn't gone out with him, he still would have put the snakes in the house. He was on the take."

She frowned. "What do you mean? Someone paid him to put those snakes in our beds? How do you know that?"

"Because he had no other reason to do it. He's not the unnamed heir. You heard the sheriff. He's not even from around here. So why would he get involved if he wasn't paid?"

"Damn, I didn't even think of that," John said. "You're right, of course. It's the only thing that makes sense. Now we just have to figure out which of the upstanding citizens of Willow Bend hired him. We've only got a couple of thousand to pick from."

"Exactly," Hunter replied. "It looks like I've got my work cut out for me."

"You're staying?" Elizabeth said, surprised.

"Of course," he said. "Even if you weren't extended family, I wouldn't leave you at the mercy of the bastards who are after the ranch. When I take on a job, I finish it."

"There's another reason he's not going anywhere," Katherine said pointedly.

"Katherine—"

At his warning tone, she gave him an innocent look. "Yes?"

"We were going to talk about this later," he reminded her. "We agreed—"

"Oh, no, *we* didn't," she argued. "That was your idea, not mine. I'd rather give you my answer now."

Watching the two of them, Elizabeth smiled. "Would one of you like to tell us what's going on?"

"No!"

"Yes," Katherine said with a grin. "Hunter asked me to marry him—"

"Are you serious! That's wonderful!"

"Congratulations! Why didn't you tell us? When's the wedding?"

Laughing as, first her sister, then John, hugged her, Katherine shrugged. "I don't know. Hunter asked me to marry him. What he didn't do was let me give him an answer."

"Why the hell not?" John demanded, scowling at his brother. "If you love her—"

"I do love her," he began.

"Yes," Katherine said.

Frowning, he tried to ignore her as he told his brother, "She hasn't had time to get over Nigel."

"I was over Nigel the second I met you," she retorted.

"I'm trying not to rush," he said, stubbornly looking anywhere except at Katherine. "I don't want to push her into a mistake."

"A mistake?" Katherine gasped. "Does this feel like

a mistake to you?" And before he could guess her intentions, she wrapped her arms around him and kissed him with all her heart.

Seconds passed, minutes. And she had to give Hunter credit—he tried to resist her blatant, shamelessly loving seduction. But she could feel the struggle going on inside of him, taste the need. Finally, with a groan, his control shattered and he kissed her back hungrily.

Lost to everything but each other, they never heard John's and Elizabeth's hoots of encouragement until they broke apart to find their respective siblings grinning at them like a couple of nuts. "Is that a yes?" Elizabeth teased.

Hunter and Katherine exchanged a look and fell into each others arms again, laughing. "Yes!"

Epilogue

The man who had done more than anyone to drive the Wyatts away from the ranch studied the calendar and bit out a curse. Time was slipping through his fingers. Enraged, he grabbed the picture off the desk in his home office and cursed the photo of Hilda Wyatt that had been taken at a church picnic years ago. Damn her! Did she really think she was going to get away with that damn will of hers? He'd see her in hell first!

She thought she was so clever, he thought furiously. But he'd outsmarted her. There were clearly any number of people who thought they were the unnamed heir in Hilda's will. And they were doing everything they could to make Buck and the rest of the Wyatts miserable.

Given the chance, they would, with time, probably drive the Wyatts away. The problem was…he couldn't afford to wait for them to accomplish what should have been a simple job. The calendar didn't lie. Where he'd had a full year, before, now he only had a matter of months to convince the Wyatts to abandon the ranch. He couldn't put his future in the hands of fools anymore. He had to take off the gloves and get down and dirty, and it wasn't going to be pretty. If the Wyatts thought they'd had trouble before, they would soon discover they hadn't seen anything yet.

Come hell or high water, the Broken Arrow would be his before the year was up.

*   *   *   *   *

Look for LAST WOLF WATCHING
by Rhyannon Byrd—
the exciting conclusion in the
BLOODRUNNERS *miniseries*
from Silhouette Nocturne.

Follow Michaela and Brody on their
fierce journey to find the truth and face
the demons from the past,
as they reach the heart of the battle
between the Runners and the rogues.

Here is a sneak preview of book three,
LAST WOLF WATCHING.

Michaela squinted, struggling to see through the impenetrable darkness. Everyone looked toward the Elders, but she knew Brody Carter still watched her. Michaela could feel the power of his gaze. Its heat. Its strength. And something that felt strangely like anger, though he had no reason to have any emotion toward her. Strangers from different worlds, brought together beneath the heavy silver moon on a night made for hell itself. That was their only connection.

The second she finished that thought, she knew it was a lie. But she couldn't deal with it now. Not tonight. Not when her whole world balanced on the edge of destruction.

Willing her backbone to keep her upright, Michaela Doucet focused on the towering blaze of a roaring bonfire that rose from the far side of the clearing, its orange flames burning with maniacal zeal against the inky black curtain of the night. Many of the Lycans had already shifted into their preternatural shapes, their fur-covered bodies standing like monstrous shadows at the edges of the forest as they waited with restless expectancy for her brother.

Her nineteen-year-old brother, Max, had been attacked by a rogue werewolf—a Lycan who preyed upon humans for food. Max had been bitten in the attack, which meant he was no longer human, but a breed of creature that existed between the two worlds of man and beast, much like the Bloodrunners themselves.

The Elders parted, and two hulking shapes emerged from the trees. In their wolf forms, the Lycans stood over seven feet tall, their legs bent at an odd angle as they stalked forward. They each held a thick chain that had been wound around their inside wrists, the twin lengths leading back into the shadows. The Lycans had taken no more than a few steps when they jerked on the chains, and her brother appeared.

Bound like an animal.

Biting at her trembling lower lip, she glanced left, then right, surprised to see that others had joined her. Now the Bloodrunners and their family and friends stood as a united force against the Silvercrest pack, which had yet to accept the fact that something sinister was eating away at its foundation—something that would rip down the protective walls that separated their world from the humans'. It occurred to Michaela that loyalties were being announced tonight—a separation made between those who would stand with the Runners in their fight against the rogues and those who blindly supported the pack's refusal to face reality. But all she could focus on was her brother. Max looked so hurt…so terrified.

"Leave him alone," she screamed, her soft-soled, black satin slip-ons struggling for purchase in the damp earth as she rushed toward Max, only to find herself lifted off the ground when a hard, heavily muscled arm clamped around her waist from behind, pulling her clear off her feet. "Damn it, let me down!" she snarled, unable to take her eyes off her brother as the golden-eyed Lycan kicked him.

Mindless with heartache and rage, Michaela clawed at the arm holding her, kicking her heels against whatever part of her captor's legs she could reach. "Stop it," a deep, husky voice grunted in her ear. "You're not helping him by losing it. I give you my word he'll survive the ceremony, but you have to keep it together."

"Nooooo!" she screamed, too hysterical to listen to reason. "You're monsters! All of you! Look what you've done to him! How dare you! *How dare you!*"

The arm tightened with a powerful flex of muscle, cinching her waist. Her breath sucked in on a sharp, wailing gasp.

"Shut up before you get both yourself and your brother killed. I will *not* let that happen. Do you understand me?" her captor growled, shaking her so hard that her teeth clicked together. "Do you understand me, Doucet?"

"Damn it," she cried, stricken as she watched one of the guards grab Max by his hair. Around them Lycans huffed and growled as they watched the spectacle, while others outright howled for the show to begin.

"That's enough!" the voice seethed in her ear. "They'll tear you apart before you even reach him, and I'll be damned if I'm going to stand here and watch you die."

Suddenly, through the haze of fear and agony and outrage in her mind, she finally recognized who'd caught her. *Brody*.

He held her in his arms, her body locked against his powerful form, her back to the burning heat of his chest. A low, keening sound of anguish tore through her, and her head dropped forward as hoarse sobs of pain ripped from her throat. "Let me go. I have to help him. *Please*," she begged brokenly, knowing only that she needed to get to Max. "Let me go, Brody."

He muttered something against her hair, his breath warm against her scalp, and Michaela could have sworn it was a single word…. But she must have heard wrong. She was too upset. Too furious. Too terrified. She must be out of her mind.

Because it sounded as if he'd quietly snarled the word *never*.

HARLEQUIN® *Romance*®

Western Weddings

Jason Welborn was convinced that his business partner's daughter, Jenny, had come to claim her share in the business. But Jenny seemed determined to win him over, and the more he tried to push her away, the more feisty Jenny's response. Slowly but surely she was starting to get under Jason's skin....

Look for

Coming Home to the Cattleman

by

JUDY CHRISTENBERRY

Available May wherever you buy books.

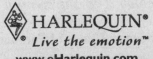

HARLEQUIN®
Live the emotion™
www.eHarlequin.com

HR17511

REQUEST YOUR FREE BOOKS!

2 FREE NOVELS PLUS 2 FREE GIFTS!

Silhouette® Romantic

SUSPENSE

Sparked by Danger, Fueled by Passion!

YES! Please send me 2 FREE Silhouette® Romantic Suspense novels and my 2 FREE gifts (gifts are worth about $10). After receiving them, if I don't wish to receive any more books, I can return the shipping statement marked "cancel." If I don't cancel, I will receive 4 brand-new novels every month and be billed just $4.24 per book in the U.S. or $4.99 per book in Canada, plus 25¢ shipping and handling per book plus applicable taxes, if any*. That's a savings of at least 15% off the cover price! I understand that accepting the 2 free books and gifts places me under no obligation to buy anything. I can always return a shipment and cancel at any time. Even if I never buy another book from Silhouette, the two free books and gifts are mine to keep forever.

240 SDN EEX6   340 SDN EEYJ

Name	(PLEASE PRINT)	
Address		Apt. #
City	State/Prov.	Zip/Postal Code

Signature (if under 18, a parent or guardian must sign)

Mail to the Silhouette Reader Service:
IN U.S.A.: P.O. Box 1867, Buffalo, NY 14240-1867
IN CANADA: P.O. Box 609, Fort Erie, Ontario L2A 5X3

Not valid to current subscribers of Silhouette Romantic Suspense books.

Want to try two free books from another line?
Call 1-800-873-8635 or visit www.morefreebooks.com.

* Terms and prices subject to change without notice. N.Y. residents add applicable sales tax. Canadian residents will be charged applicable provincial taxes and GST. This offer is limited to one order per household. All orders subject to approval. Credit or debit balances in a customer's account(s) may be offset by any other outstanding balance owed by or to the customer. Please allow 4 to 6 weeks for delivery. Offer available while quantities last.

Your Privacy: Silhouette is committed to protecting your privacy. Our Privacy Policy is available online at www.eHarlequin.com or upon request from the Reader Service. From time to time we make our lists of customers available to reputable third parties who may have a product or service of interest to you. If you would prefer we not share your name and address, please check here. ☐

SRS08

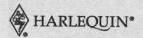

HARLEQUIN®

American ★ Romance®

Three Boys and a Baby

When Ella Garvey's eight-year-old twins and
their best friend, Dillon, discover an abandoned
baby girl, they fear she will be put in jail—
or worse! They decide to take matters into their
own hands and run away. Luckily the outlaws are
found quickly…and Ella finds a second chance
at love—with Dillon's dad, Jackson.

LOOK FOR

Three Boys and a Baby

BY

LAURA MARIE ALTOM

Available May
wherever you buy books.

LOVE, HOME & HAPPINESS

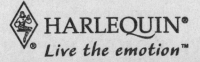

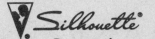
Silhouette®
Romantic
SUSPENSE

COMING NEXT MONTH